Books by Lindsay Hill

fiction

Sea of Hooks

poetry

Avelaval

Archaeology

Kill Series

NdjenFerno

Contango

The Empty Quarter

Tidal Lock

a novel by

Lindsay Hill

PM

McPherson & Company

Kingston, New York

This is solely and completely a work of fiction.
Designed by Bruce R. McPherson
Published by McPherson & Company,
Post Office Box 1126, Kingston, New York 12402
www.mcphersonco.com

FIRST EDITION
978-1620540633

1 3 5 7 9 10 8 6 4 2 2024 2025 2126 2027

MANUFACTURED IN THE U.S.A.

Library of Congress Cataloging-in-Publication Data

Names: Hill, Lindsay, 1952- author.
Title: Tidal lock / a novel by Lindsay Hill.
Description: First edition. | Kingston, New York : McPherson & Company, 2024. |
Identifiers: LCCN 2024023102 (print) | LCCN 2024023103 (ebook) | ISBN 9781620540633 (hardcover) | ISBN 9781620540657 (epub)
Subjects: LCGFT: Novels.
Classification: LCC PS3558.I395 T53 2024 (print) | LCC PS3558.I395 (ebook) | DDC 813/.54—dc23/eng/20240517
LC record available at https://lccn.loc.gov/2024023102
LC ebook record available at https://lccn.loc.gov/2024023103

Grateful acknowledgement to *New England Review*,
where a selection of these passages first appeared.

Tidal Lock

For Nita

I

The Shred-Paper River

DISAPPEARED

Cats that disappear are usually close by I read somewhere—but something switched in them—switched off or on—and now you're a predator they think—so you can call them but they won't come out. Other things are like that too. If you get a map of your neighborhood—or draw one yourself—and then make a circle X feet from your house—your cat is inside that circle they say—but you won't find your cat I think because you have completely forgotten how to look among all the things like shrubs and shadows and stairways you're used to not looking at really. I don't have a cat. I stole a map of the west because my father disappeared and I wanted to draw a circle to find him in but what's the scale—what's the conversion rate between cats and people—I don't think anyone knows exactly. I ran my fingers down the spine of the Sierras—it was like dousing rods or a Ouija Board—I was waiting for some heat or magnetism—some pull from underneath.

My name is sometimes Olana. I like to draw things and steal things and go into buildings slated for demolition. Things on the map I stole are not where I used to think they were. Things are like that a lot I've noticed lately.

DEMOLITIONS

Dust from the demolitions clouds the world—gathers in houses—on doorsteps—in the corners of rooms—advances on streets in side-winding wisps. It must be swept out and swept and swept out. Where will it go but into the air to settle again in a different place? It must be swept out every morning and during the day and even at night before sleep and my thoughts about my father are just like that. Other things in my life are like that too—regrets are like that too and I sweep them out with my words—out of the corners of my life where they stack up—where hours blow them into heaps—where thinking turns them in spirals like tornadoes that climb and widen.

Dr. Winker says I have a *melancholic miasma*. To me this sounds like some sorry valve in your heart that doesn't work—or a vine-clogged swamp—nothing gets through is the point—like that time I put pretty much the whole lasagna a friend had made for me—when I was sick and staying at her place—down the garbage disposal in her kitchen sink—when she went out—because the mushrooms were like eating ears and the tomato sauce tasted like the metal can I used to keep my marbles in.

NEEDLES

The last time I saw my father I barely saw him. Now that morning seems sharp as shears but I know it wasn't. I was half-asleep. I think I made my way to the kitchen. I think my father was already starting to leave. We may have hugged. He said a thing or two that I don't remember. I never saw him again. It's one thing when someone dies and you think of them and miss them. Everyone knows it's not the same when someone's still alive and you don't know where they are or why they left or what's become of them—and do they think of you at all—and what are they doing right now while you're thinking of them—and you're thinking of them again and again. I let my fingers walk down the Sierras—past Mono Lake—into Yosemite—into Death Valley—that's the place all right—you're dead before you even know you're thirsty so I've heard. What kind of name for a town is *Needles* anyway?

MIRROR OF THE DEAD

I saw a gray mirror once in an auction house—antique—free standing—full length—gray like a shell I'd found at Siren Beach—more luminous than reflective—more murky. The mirrors of the dead look just like that I thought. I mean the dead are to the living as that mirror is to mirrors—which means the dead don't work the way the living do—they don't work the way that mirror—gray and lustered and milky—doesn't work as a mirror—which means you can't see anything in it really—you can't find yourself in it—you can't find the room where you stand—everything blurred and indefinite—that's the kind of reflection the mirror of the dead throws back because that's what being dead is like—I'm sure.

Do you think the dead can love more fiercely than the living—alive to loss as they are—being dead—alive to every foothold being fragile—the taken for granted hold you have on things—every taken for granted handhold in the world—like the way the living can fiercely love the dead but in reverse? Nothing is taken for granted by the dead. To love like that is what I'm thinking of.

I like to walk by the sea. I like to pick up shells—driftwood and feathers—to put in the pockets of my coat with the things I've found in shops that I want for a second or two and take. The ocean is a house the size of time—a house with no rooms—the way time has no rooms really—the way the self has no rooms beneath its welter of walls—down deep—where the mirrors of the dead cast light without limit—where gray waves thrust forward. You know the self is not a shore. You know because people drown there nearly all the time. You've seen this—maybe even in yourself.

I'm a romantic I guess—meaning I think there's something behind all of this—that all of this stands for something—points to something—has music behind it—something like that—something shining through from behind—not that music shines—not really—but you know what I mean—when the wind is twisting your hair and you start to spin with your eyes closed by the sea with your arms held out—shining like that.

THROWING ROCKS AND LIGHTING FIRES

My father was thirty-nine when he disappeared. I was thirteen. This was years ago. I don't know how many. The woman who sometimes says she is my mother says he died. She doesn't know anything. Losing someone you love who's still alive is like being locked out of your own house. You are going from window to window and you are trying every door and at first you are disbelieving and then you are self-reproachful and then you are seething—so angry and displaced—and you want to start breaking windows and breaking down doors and throwing rocks and lighting fires and just burning the place to the ground.

I sit very quietly sometimes—very still—like someone stunned. I sit very still—sometimes looking out to sea—sometimes on a bench in a park—sometimes I lie on my back and look at the stars. The stars aren't visible mostly but sometimes they are and I lie on my back and the size of the sky and the distances comfort me. The mirror of the dead is in my room—in a corner—you wouldn't believe how cheap a mirror is that doesn't work.

SCISSOR DAY

I call the day my father left me *Scissor Day*. Every Scissor Day I cut to pieces the thing that matters most to me. So Scissor Day is a holiday in reverse—a reversal of the engine that drives the world—the engine of acquisition. I started with all the photos of my father. I scissored them to bits and bits and smaller and smaller bits. You have two earrings and you lose one and you know that all you ever had was one and one and that two never was at all. You lose a person from your life and you know that two is not a unity of things but just things positioned side by side and positioning isn't solid like a stone in your hand that you strike against a stone to make a spark it's circumstantial and brief and two is just a separation in the making because there are only just ones and it's like being locked out of your own house I told you but there's nothing you can break to get inside—no doors—no windows—nothing you can break that makes a difference. There's only everything inside you—loose—flailing and battering like bridge cables uncoupled in hurricanes reaching out and coiling back and lashing the air and battering the very bridge they've once held up.

THE HOLDER

The woman who comes to the house—the one I told you sometimes says she is my mother—I call her *the holder* because she holds me here—this roof over my head—scant food—a few coins now and then like what you'd spare a beggar on the street. Have you ever closed your hand around a moth very slowly until its wings are tucked tight against it so tight that it cannot even move and did you notice how it does not any longer try to move how it doesn't resist anymore it's just being still in your closed hand? I don't remember who she actually is. She's common as coats and keys—dull as a trowel. Don't even bother to talk about anything important—coats and keys and chairs and cars and light bulbs—stuff like that is all she's got. Anything else she blinks like waking in glare—anything else she turns away like smoke blown in her face. She's not who she says she is. I know. I've followed her. She says she teaches school. She doesn't. She wanders her life like a person with a metal detector at the beach. I think she lost a daughter and can't accept it. Now she keeps me.

BUTTONS

I swept the dust from my room again today. I swept it from the street in front of the house. Blond ruins—weightless remnants of what once weighed on everyone—of all that required lifting and carrying and bearing forward—of all that had to be hefted in the transport toward the ever more gigantic. Now there is only the minimal—this minimal—this minimal mixture of air and disintegrated greatness—the reminders and the reminded—the bristles of a broom against bare floor.

I've learned you should pay attention to things you've always loved. Even as a child I used to go into the closet and cut buttons from the coats of guests and hide them in my room and later take them out and spread them out and how beautiful and magical and hard like a sheet of music they were when laid out in uneven lines. I cut them with the double-edged razor from my father's shaving kit—very carefully—and tried not to cut myself—holding only the dull side-edges—and never ever put the razor in my pocket and forget that it was there and reach in and then my pocket would be full of blood.

These things that persist—in your life—you have to pay attention to these things—these things that stay with you. They don't back off—you can't scare them back—they aren't like skittish creatures huddled on the margins of a clearing you've made in the woods to set up camp and set up chairs and build a fire or whatever people do out there with that camping stuff—poles and tarps and Bunsen burners and beakers and dried peas—it's not science—this isn't about hit or miss or mixing compounds or how does someone decide what goes with what to replicate a result that someone else had some luck with—this is about *taking hold—being taken hold of.*

INTENTIONS

I don't know why *the holder* comes to the house with groceries—leaves them—then leaves. Intentions are like cats that hide when you look for them. I know she opposes Scissor Days. I'm sure of that. You cannot stop Scissor Days. You cannot oppose the gods without consequence. Over time I converted the coins to bills and horded them—just in case she tires of me and stops coming around. You understand.

NEEDLES

I'm trying to picture it. I think it must be like being under a rock—a whole town under a rock—because being lost in Needles and being in Needles are just the same thing. Look on the map—look where it is—it's a disappearing bag in the desert—the bag you crawl into from that children's book and no one can see you in there. In Needles everyone is in that bag together—I just know it—and I know it's not the kind of place where people go by their real names. It's the kind of place people go when the life their real name stood for is that broken thing you keep but can't use anymore.

DOUBLING

Do you ever try things on? I don't mean clothes—I mean being another person. It was late and I was tired. My father and I had been traveling all day—walking through towns—browsing—window shopping—resting on benches here and there—grabbing a bite to eat—migrating back to train stations—leaving. As children we all made cardboard houses that we could live in. Boxes from the store or storage rooms or found on sidewalks next to garbage cans. We built those houses—made worlds—easy as hopscotch—jump rope—jacks. My father called it *doubling*. It meant you could be someone else—at least for a while—a kind of pretending that crosses over and then you're not pretending anymore—like when you first went to school and were pretending to be a student until you got what that meant and then you were a student even though that wasn't who you'd been when you entered the school but now you were—at least you were when you were there. Others around you were doubling as students too except those who couldn't or didn't and those were the ones who were in trouble all the time. Sometimes you chose to be in trouble but for some this was not a choice—they were in trouble all the time—because they could not double. Many things are like that in life I think—that time the history teacher slammed the yardstick across my desk to break my gaze out the window onto the sky where its history lesson of all things moving and forming and pulling apart and dissolving was playing out.

My father said having a single identity was like building a house around you with no doors. So doubling wasn't lying exactly. It was just a way to find a way out of yourself. It's not like that time I asked that man on the corner for directions to a street I knew did not exist because I wanted to see how people can't be seen as not knowing something and he gave me directions that he knew I couldn't follow like the ones I gave my cousin for making butter and I didn't know how to make butter and I just told her to put everything she could find in the kitchen in a bowl and mix it by hand for an hour.

Or that other time when that friend asked if I knew how to make butter because that was her homework assignment and her father said he'd take us bowling once her homework was done. I was younger and a liar not because I wanted to be a liar or even thought much about it but you know how you're just made a certain way so some things you're just pretty good at right away well for me that was lying. Anyway I told that friend all the things that went into making butter and she wrote them down in her perfect handwriting and it was all properly punctuated and above the line except the letters that dipped below the line but not too far below the line because that's the kind of person that friend was—a not-too-far-below-the-line kind of person—and she was naturally that way the way I was naturally a liar and anyway we didn't get to go bowling that day and my friend was not happy with me and it was only just the first in a series of unhappinesses—like an unhappy advent calendar because behind every little door she opened was another lie and when that friend needed to know how to make pumpkin spice that fall she didn't even ask me if I knew how to make it and I never really liked that friend much after that.

TRAINS

We were on a train. *I write and self-publish educational pamphlets for children* my father said to the proper mother and little girl sitting across from us in the compartment—like *How to know when you're bleeding—How to know when you're drowning—How to know when you're lost in a dark woods in winter and about to starve—I think I might have a sample here somewhere* he continued—leaning toward the child and digging around in his briefcase—*Would you like one?* The girl had that quiver-lipped look of being about to be handed off to an uncle she didn't remember. The mother came down like a cleaver—*I'd rather she didn't.* My father mustered his most wounded softest voice—*I wrote them to save lives you know.*

PERFECTION

I've heard when you go through a doorway you forget. You go into a room and you've forgotten why—you look for hints—something was urgent—it's here in this room somewhere—what was it—your brain is blank as boards. I don't remember that much about my mother. I think we were mixed math—decimals and fractions trying to talk to each other. If I talked about the stars—the galaxies—the size of everything beyond—she talked about the weather. Even living in the same house—walking the same floors—eating the same food—we couldn't stop opposing one another—like scissor-blades chopping all that lies between them into bits.

My mother wanted everything to be perfect. I remember that. She kept books for a bunch of businesses—perfect like that. And I remember how she'd fish the longest extension cord we had out of a crate of extension cords and plug it into an outside outlet and plug the vacuum cleaner into the extension cord—the vacuum we used in the house—and go into the front yard and vacuum the fluffy seedpods from the heads of the dandelions and I asked if she'd at least wear a bathrobe and a medical bracelet while doing this but of course she wouldn't. Finally my mother liked things to be final. In that way that self-reliant people like final things. In that way that things can't be final so you cut them short. So she was always cutting things short that could not be finished—like that self-reliant woman I read about who tried to take her own tonsils out with a wood burning kit and a mirror—you know—that wood burning kit your parents wouldn't let you have because you were too young or too clumsy or you could have one later or next year when you knew how to hold fiery things or sharp things all because you'd stapled yourself to your homework that time and had to get a tetanus shot.

Even cats are instinctively reluctant to step through doorways—everyone with a cat has witnessed this. Something pulls them back—some risk—some danger undetermined. Almost always they mark the doorway first—with a brush of the cheek—before going through—wanting that sure way back that cats require. Even a cat knows the cost of not remembering where you are.

I don't know what happened to my mother after she left—or we left her—whichever it was—those times my father swept me away on trains to save my life he said. Maybe she declared us perfectly dead and married an actuary. Something pulled her out I know—like coffee pulls you out of the train wreck of morning—or that time you pulled yourself out of quicksand by pulling someone else in. The thing about perfection is how final it is—how there's no place to go from there. So everything got to that place of nowhere to go. Then she was gone.

Some people can do that I've noticed. Just leave with their life and that's that. I've never left anything that way I think you know by now if you've paid attention. I don't know why people marry each other anyway. Maybe each puts their best aspect on display and each assumes there must be more. I've had that experience over and over again while buying bacon.

TRAINS

Sometimes on trains we'd have to pull onto a siding *to let the world go by* as my father called it—huge long freight trains pulling coal and oil and lumber—trains pulling real things—things that were their actual sizes inside and out—not like people with worlds the sizes of stars inside their heads—the sizes of galaxies—not things mostly full of myths and maps—you know—real things—things like fuels and load-bearing beams. These things went by a lot on train after train—all the things that underpinned our journeys—these rode rapidly past where we waited to roll like coins across tabletops—toward and over edges—maybe getting lost or getting found—picked up by someone else—circulated differently through the world—another path like atoms exchanging themselves into other things.

DESTINATIONS

Everyone in Needles is missing from somewhere else—at least that's the way I imagine it—what do you think—what do you think people do when they're crossing the desert and they can't go any further—*I'll just stop here* they say to themselves—that's what they do—that story of the man lost in the snow and he tries to lure his dog to kill and bury his frozen hands in its hot insides but the dog catches on and keeps its distance and the man can't go any further and he lies down to sleep a bit—and says to himself that he'll just lie down for a while—and he never wakes up—so you are in the desert and you can't go on so you'll just stop here for a bit—between destinations—and then you notice that between destinations is where you'll never be found.

ANTICIPATION

The best part about seeing my friend is looking forward to it. She lives at *The Castaways* apartments—a decrepit nautical affair with peeled paint and broken-out first floor windows. She's the last one there—gets eviction notices—ignores them. I think being evicted is just too much like *going somewhere* to suit her. Befriending my friend is like getting a leech to treat your attachment disorder. Today she thinks maybe she got bitten by a sea snake—she says *It's one of the worst you know.* She says she may not make it. She's not going to talk about it much more unless it gets much worse she says. She sends me out to find a tourniquet though. Mostly friendship is something you seek then seek to escape I've noticed—the way fame is for some. I didn't know my friend had ever even once been in the sea.

MANNEQUIN

The holder speaks intimacy as a non-native language—words like ice cubes instead of words like rivers—or when a mannequin hugs you from behind and it's not quite right. She lost her daughter at some carnival I think it was—took her eyes off her for a moment near the cotton candy machine or the whiffle-throw or something like that and she was gone—gone in an instant—the way some things go—just like that—and then they're gone for good. I had a friend who said she was a reincarnated carny—not a big improvement in her case. The teeth like flint corn—the loose fast gangly way of speaking—all tendrils and tight corners—the slightly attractive dangerous good looks if there'd been some breeding—one of them snatched that girl—or one of the people loitering and looking for something to snatch. You don't want to imagine the things that happened next but you can't help it—you know—you start prying at that cavity under the gumline and you can't stop—the pain so pure electrical and fresh. Anyway the woman needed a kind of daughter substitute so that's what happened. Like the time I lost a tooth playing tether ball when I was maybe nine and it was down there in the gravel somewhere and I couldn't find it and I was on my knees digging around and the other kids were laughing and still playing and the ball was whizzing around and the kids were practically stepping over me so I just gave up and picked up a piece of gravel that looked like a tooth and put it under my pillow and the tooth fairy was fooled and left a coin or two. It was that sort of thing with her I think. She found me at the school or maybe at the market and we started playing the mother daughter game and whatever gods govern such things were fooled so I sort of became her daughter in a way.

CRAZY

I'm not crazy you know. Some people play at being crazy and they rock back and forth and look at the ceiling and spin their hair with their fingers and speak in a wispy faraway voice and want to be exempt from the rules of the road and the rules of two feet on the ground and then when something's at stake for them they lock into place like the parts of a freshly cleaned pistol and they get really sharp and pointed and acute and adroit and on top of everything and *where did that come from* you want to ask but you know where it came from it came from that current of self-interest running under them like the electric floor of a bumper car rink. I've never been crazy like that.

DR. WINKER

I call my therapist Dr. Winker because he has a kind of nervous tic where he smiles then winks involuntarily from time to time. So you're telling him about some trauma like the time you tried to cut the thick stubborn cardboard boxes with your father's recently unruly folding knife to make the walls of a secret room behind the luggage in the basement—stitches lots of stitches—and he smiles and winks like he gets the inside joke of your life and wants you to know for sure that he gets it. His office is in the Pharaoh Building—the one downtown with the hieroglyphs embossed in gold on the lobby walls and the little closed pharmacy and the elevator out of service so I have to take the stairs. There's never anyone waiting in Dr. Winker's waiting room so what kind of room is it really?

MYSTERY SHOPPER

My friend pointed out that your car battery is never dead until you want to start your car. A lot of things are that way in life I think. I think *the holder* wants me to get a job. She brings it up again and again like cud. Flying kites is always a travesty in my experience. All that hope-fueled running and flinging to no purpose whatsoever. I heard about this thing called *mystery shopping*. *What's the mystery* I wondered. Turns out to just be someone pretending to be a customer and telling on people and getting paid. More like everyday life than a mystery it seems to me—making a buck by pretending to be someone you're not at the expense of someone else.

TRAINS

We traveled all day through Sweden by train to Lake Ostesund and my father was hungry and I was tired and he went off to eat at a restaurant and a couple began to sort of flirt with him and the wife was beautiful and silent and the husband talked incessantly and some soft music was playing and the husband said to my father *She wants to dance with you* and they danced and she kissed him softly on the lips and then they invited him to come to their house for the night and what if he'd accepted and one thing had led to another and the three of them had really fallen in love and then traveled to Norway and south to Denmark and then to Morocco and rented a rambling house pressed against the mountains and the years had gone by in a blur of tea and smoke and spicy lamb and I'd never seen him again and I'd awakened from my nap and had nowhere to look for him and I was desperate and searching and I didn't ever forget him but I didn't ever find him and his life was just so sweet that all that had gone before just didn't hold him and not being in touch became a habit and then a preference and then a necessity and I grew old and imagined him long dead and the last time I saw him I was just lying down on an ordinary afternoon to take a nap.

BROKEN SIDEWALKS

I don't know how to pay attention mostly. I trip over broken sidewalks—skin my knees—sprain my wrists—just my body getting in the way again—of what I'm trying to do—of finding what I'm looking for—just not able to take care of itself when I'm trying to think. You know what I mean—all those times you've cut yourself cutting onions—peeling potatoes—because you weren't really in the room you were ahead of yourself somewhere on some sidewalk seeking something.

FINGERNAIL TYPE THINGS

Do you ever think of all the fingernail type things—things you take for granted but you don't know where they come from or how they work or what they really are? What is baking soda anyway—maybe it mostly comes from shaken out shoes or something—and how about all those rubber bands that make it into the house somehow—things you neither choose nor ever run out of—like desires. You can't keep track of all the things you can't explain so they rot in heaps somewhere outside your thoughts like all that stuff thrown out the back door of that house across the street where those people who want to keep what they throw away live with the shades pulled down and smoke coming from the chimney even when it's hot.

EEL

My friend is effervescent and inert—like a dozing electric eel. She went to one of those schools for making handmade musical instruments and felt and dolls. It was almost too rigorous for her. I had some business cards made for her birthday—*self-unemployed* they said.

PAIN

I was in the watch district when I fell today. I sat on the curb—torn beneath my clothes—rolling up my pants to assess the damage. I don't think I was crying but I wanted to. I hoped the pain was making me better the way it's supposed to—the way you learned as a child—almost first thing—that when you're in pain—whatever it is—it's working. When I skinned my knee trying to take the neighbor kid's bike away to hide so they'd think it was stolen and get in trouble for leaving it out my mother applied that spray stuff that stung like boiling acid and when I shrieked she said *that's how you know it's working* so then I knew that when I was in pain whatever it was was working.

THINGS THAT SLIP THROUGH YOUR FINGERS

Things that slip through your fingers are never gone it seems to me—you never stop looking for them—you never stop almost having them—even when walking broken streets—even while working with knives. Trying to figure out what happened to my father year after year is like shuffling the same deck of cards over and over where you have something different every time but you have nothing new again and again. Sometimes I stretch out on the broad irregular earth—look at the great night sky—let everything inside rise and move away—like exhaling under water.

DEAD HORSE

I've heard you can beat a dead horse but you can't make it drink. Like that time I told my neighbor about the treasure map I'd found with the X in the middle of their basement floor and if they didn't mind could I just poke around down there a bit—no jackhammers or anything like that—just see if there was some evidence to be found and they showed their gratitude by calling my parents and saying I had a problem that should be looked at by a professional and that was the first I'd heard about people who make a life of looking into problems people are having and I wondered if some day I might be a person like that but I wasn't.

CASTAWAYS

I've known some people I think the dead love better than. You too I bet. My friend is like one of those naps that makes you feel like you've given three quarts of blood and then got handed a cup of orange juice. When she moved to The Castaways it went like this—while I was unloading the truck and lugging the boxes up the stairs—she was managing to tinker with the vacuum cleaner —holding the tubes up to the light—*I think there's a hairball in here somewhere* she said. Now she was sitting on the floor—defeated—all the pieces lying around her like the parts of toys a petulant child has pulled from a long disregarded toy box—all that pointy discombobulation soon to be abandoned as it was now time for tea or so she reasoned and she rose and went to the kitchen and got distracted and started opening boxes getting interested in whether there were sufficient matching knives and forks and spoons for a decent table setting and soon they were in stacks with the non-matching pieces set aside—*I don't think we can make much of this* she muttered absently and all the while I was lugging the boxes and she was the one who seemed to be exhausted. Later she tripped over one of the vacuum hoses and then her bruised big toe needed attention—she insisted on mercurochrome—of which of course there was none—because she said it was the color of healing—and then she had to get snippy and lie on the couch with her foot elevated while I unpacked the boxes and put all her stuff away. I told my friend she wasn't the nicest person in the world and she said *most people aren't.*

Maybe you think who your friends are tells you all you need to know about yourself. I don't. Sometimes you have friends the way people have apartments—the best they can afford. You have friends that aren't too costly—I don't mean money you know I don't mean costly like that—I mean cost you the things that mean the most to you—so you can have friends who don't even know you and maybe they're the best kinds of friends to have because they can't cost you a thing.

LIAR

Memory is like having a working dog that works against you. Dr. Winker says I'm not a liar—I just can't tell what happened from what didn't. I think he thinks he's reassuring me—as if origami were some lesser art—as if what happens isn't mostly flat—like paper on a table—and you just make it into something more interesting and what's wrong with that? I guess you think because you can't rely on an origami bird to fly you think there's something wrong and well you're just so literal aren't you and what's that gotten you so far anyway I want to know.

CRUMB-TRAY FIRES

When my friend has me clean her kitchen—I don't get *paid* you understand—she never fails to remind me that toaster crumb-tray fires cost lives. She's over on the couch—wanding me around with flicks of her wrist and vague pointing gestures—*I think you missed a spot—Don't forget the toaster crumb-tray—those fires cost lives you know.* I'm thinking she can clean her own crumb-tray but she's the kind of person if you ask her to do anything—even something that benefits her—she says *I didn't ask to be born.* That's the kind of person she was and I was the kind of person who would have that kind of person for a friend which doesn't speak very highly of me so what.

Just so you know—three quarts of blood is half the blood you have.

TILTING

Dr. Winker wants me to reach for a *better me* I think it is. Those prizes they used to put in cereal boxes—in the days before choking hazards—those little plastic toy prizes at the bottoms of the boxes and you'd tilt the box after tearing it open and tilt it more and reach down over all that tilted cereal but you'd always tilt it too far so the cereal started to spill out and you were reaching farther and farther like a farmer trying to bring a breach-birth calf into the world and it was a paradigm you couldn't shake in your life where something was promised and it was buried at the bottom of something else—at the bottom of a relationship—or with that passing grade buried in that teacher somewhere—and you had to have a strategy for retrieving it—that thing you wanted—and it always involved some form of tilting—tilting your point of view to see the other person in some positive light or tilting your life into the night to finish that paper because the person you were working with—the one who was smarter than you and you were counting on them to help you—I mean write the paper for you—got theirs done early and went to a late movie with some popular kids who were living on another spectrum of grading and looked down from those radiant peaks where lightning lit the sky but never struck them down at least not until after high school.

LIAR

Dr. Winker says I'm *not a liar*. Beneath a twitch of sympathy I sense a hint of taint when he tells me this—as if the wooden world were all that's worth remembering—as if the imagined generates no origins—as if revelation corresponds to lived experience—as if the past were a prison you put on lockdown after a break or a riot.

SCISSOR DAYS

I don't know how many Scissor Days there've been. Every day is the anniversary of someone missing. So Scissor Day became any day I loved something the most—the way my father started celebrating his birthday whenever he wanted—sometimes many times in a single year—sometimes twice a month—and you run out of things to give and you run out of things to say and you run out of ways to celebrate.

The last time I saw my father was on a train. The floors of the house are bare and bright as stars. You're always in the middle of someone being lost—nowhere to start. You take the life you've been handed at face value—without question—the way you buy cornflakes or cornstarch—the way you shop for basics.

THE SQUARE OF NOTHING

I give my own names to things because mostly names are applied like price tags—applied without listening and weighing the true nature of a thing—applied like numbers on houses to make some sense of the pretty much senseless. Nothing has only one name. Think of the parallel opposites called *the sea.* I give my own names to things because settling for the names you inherit is like settling for the life you are handed in the assembly line of lives. I call the great empty square at the city's center *The Square of Nothing.* Great umber colonnades line its borders. Shop fronts—once fashionable—now boarded up. There is no fountain—no monument—there is nothing at the center. No one walks across it. Everyone skirts its edges on their way to somewhere else.

DEMOLITIONS

Dust from the demolitions is in my hair and I don't want to wash it out—it crowds the streets—clogs the downspouts—clogs the storm drains—rests on people's shoulders—on people's shoes. No one bothers to brush it off anymore—it fills every empty space—piles into corners—burns the eyes like smoke but people are used to it. Some of the dust is data—the ground-to-bits statistics once housed in buildings—the measures—the metrics—the calculus of outcomes—it has the feel of scouring powder between your fingers—as if you could scrub your fingerprints right off if you just stayed with it. The newspaper distribution boxes on corners are filled with dust. I lift their see-through fronts and the dust slides onto my feet. This is the only news of the demolitions—otherwise unreported—unmentioned.

I saw them walking on Tuck Street. The mother looked pained-and-trying-to-be-optimistic like someone with adult orthodontics. Her being-dragged-along-behind-her-child was screaming *I don't want to be buried—I don't want to be buried* but she couldn't notice.

These people you never see again—what happens to them—maybe they combust—their ashes spread with the dust—maybe you breathe those ashes in and their lostness propels your blood.

SCISSORS

Things divided. Things split to pairs. Things that are one and two at the same time like scissors. Maybe that's why they disappear—scissors I mean—because they can't agree with themselves. Maybe people are like that too and people who disappear disappear because they can't agree with themselves and the only way to be a single thing and not agree with yourself is to disappear—the way scissors do—where even when you have your special drawer for them they're not in that drawer and where are they—you won't ever figure it out. They aren't in the pillowcases hiding with the missing socks—they aren't in the drawer you forget you have because there's nothing in that drawer that you ever need—the way seventh grade was nothing you ever needed so you can't remember it really—or maybe just a slide or two like after a fire a few slides survived in a metal box while the rest were lost.

DEMOLITIONS

No one knows who conducts the demolitions. Notices are sometimes placed on buildings—often not. I am not going to tell you this more than once—not only the edges of the city are being demolished—the industrial edges where things were stamped and assembled—demolitions have moved into neighborhoods—the dust is in every street—people have grown used to this as children grow used to cruel parents who intrude and control so the child can hardly breathe. You cannot know at all the way out of this. Hell is not full of flames—it's beige.

TIDAL LOCK

As they say in that *for-your-own-good* safety announcement at the tilt-a-whirl—*thank you for listening*. You're impatient I guess to know what city I'm in—how I got here—what I'm doing here. The unfamiliar is hard—it is—but it's so much harder to find your way in the almost-familiar—those pieces lying around that used to be that thing you built that barely worked so why are you trying so hard to put it back together when it's finally fallen apart?

Did you ever feel like you didn't live in a real place? Maybe not. I call this city *Tidal Lock*. I'm looking for my father or what happened to him.

I don't think I've always lived here. Sometimes you can't find a way to ask the question of how you got somewhere—ask it in a way that it can be answered. Some things come from where you've not been looking. Some come from far off and are visible for miles—for years—but you don't have a way to stop them—to step out of their way—to move to the side in your life—to get out of the way of that thing you've seen coming all along.

Some things you learn. Some things you never learn. Sometimes something in your architecture keeps you circling back the same old way that wrecked you last time and the time before—something in the way you were made that you can't decide against. You tried to sharpen knives because your father asked you to. It seemed simple as hanging a door. No one just hangs a door or sharpens knives. You think you can do these things but they must be learned. Some things you cannot learn and you have to learn this about yourself. You have to wall yourself off from choosing these things if you can—know you will otherwise be trying to fit doors into walls again and again—again and again you will pick up knives to sharpen.

I'm telling you I don't know where I lived before I lived here. As if you were to wake in that house by the slicing river waters and you were trying to remember where you'd been—even the day before—but the sound of that river was like paper being shredded and your memories were ribbons before you could start to read them and the sound of that shred-paper river displaced the past and became your origin.

YOUR PAST

Sometimes a part of your life—a part of your past—breaks off and crashes down and lands in your path—and it's huge next to every-thing grown suddenly small beside it. The way the over-weighted shelves of your day crash into your sleep with all their disarranged tumbling-down contents banging their way through your night show.

LOCKED-ROOM MYSTERY

I find you in that locked-room mystery of sleep—standing empty as a doorway—maybe the doorway you went through when you forgot the world. Tides tear side-by-side like angry hands when something's over. You can't imagine the pull at both sides of me—the back-and-forth force of it. Or I'm on fire and breaking apart like debris against the atmosphere and the hours are combusting beside me and I do not look back because I cannot look back because in a locked-room dream you can only look for that impossible way to get out. I wake engaged like a bike chain wakes when its person starts to pedal.

TRAINS

The last time I saw my father was on a train. We were in Barcelona leaving to go south down the coast. He'd left something in the station—I can't remember what—and he rushed off the train and he was yelling something over his shoulder as he ran and I couldn't understand what it was and I couldn't gather my things fast enough to catch up with him before the train pulled out and I couldn't throw myself off the train just to be with him.

WAITING

When you walk through the city you will see them—those who are waiting—looking absently around—uncomfortable in that particular way that though they are completely experienced at it they have never grown used to it—a kind of fated slightly hopeful look that carries beneath it the apprehension that those for whom they wait may never come. Often they have brought something to read or have ordered a beverage—maybe a glass of wine if late in the day—that they don't really want—a kind of rent on the space they use to wait—and wait. The one who waits is always the one with more at stake in being there. Why else would they wait? Those they wait for are otherwise occupied—busy—excited—engaged—those they wait for are in the middle of their lives while those who wait are always on the margins—and that is the look now that I think about it—that is the discomfort you can't get used to—being on the margins for having kept your word while those who failed to keep theirs are in the middle of their lives.

PROMOTION

The cable car going up the hill never operates. I think there was a restaurant up there that went out of business. Or a skating rink that went out of business or a bar—a bar with lots of sports and tables and table-sports I seem to remember. Maybe they'll have a re-grand opening sometime—maybe with a promotion I could design—*All you can eat or your money back*—something along those lines.

DUST

Today I'm in the industrial district taking notes. *Typhoon Fasteners* —its plant long derelict—now uncoupled from its use—what was made here—now unneeded. I trace a map of the west in industrial dust. The tips of my fingers shimmer like glittery lakes in tiny landscapes lit by an overhead sun. I touch them to my tongue—one by one—as if parched.

You make of this what you will. I make of it what I can. What I can make of it is this—I want to taste whatever sends light back to its source—I want to taste whatever shimmers housed in dust. I want to take the shaken-down world onto my tongue. I want to press its caustic remnants against the roof of my mouth.

POISONED

My friend says she has fish-tooth-food-poisoning for sure. *Think about it* she implores as she heads to the bathroom—*you leave fish out in 100 degree weather for eight hours and then you eat it and what happens*—after she comes out—wiping her mouth—she continues—*so you have that fish from last night's dinner stuck between your teeth all night and its almost 100 degrees in there and then that fish gets dislodged by your tongue or something and you swallow it and no surprise you are sick to the point of wishing you were dead and that's what's happening to me and maybe I'll need plasma or something if it doesn't get better almost right away.*

MOTHS

I prefer the smell of moths to the smell of mothballs. So much is like that I think.

UNPROFESSIONAL BUILDING

I walk past the now abandoned *Unprofessional Building* on Flat Street—at least that's what I used to call it—you know—for people who wanted to save some money by using an amateur dentist—you know—a hobbyist—or if you just needed some stitches—a few—not on your face—maybe on the inside of your leg or something—something to do with a falling jackknife maybe—that got away from you—or you had a little hair fire—or a problem with a penknife you were sharpening in your palm—or a fireplace poker minor eye accident—or if your arm was just a little broken.

TRACKS

Along the railroad tracks the air sometimes sparkles like thrown glitter when the trains make songs high and shrill as whistles blown to bring the secret animals out from where they hide in the undergrowth watching and waiting sometimes whole lifetimes for a moment to intervene on your behalf against your thoughtlessness. I had hoped the tracks would lead out of town but always somewhere north of counting tie after tie I lost my thread and wandered into some district unfamiliar or unremembered and always there were doors off hinges and glassless window frames and desks with drawers thrown open and contents thrown around as if rifled by tornadoes the size of children's busy busy fingers.

THE MAN IN THE DOORWAY

A man stood in the doorway of a closed tobacconist—every day. He was nondescript as sand but I noticed him. I saw him clearly—meek and small and plain as sand. I noticed him. Others didn't—rivers eddying sand bars—blind like that. He was nondescript but I saw him. I knew he was waiting for someone. He was small. His face was formless and soft—as if fashioned from gray clay. The kind of face you can't remember really. His clothes seemed out of place—I don't mean anachronistic exactly—I mean as if from some almost-recent dustbowl era—small-city business clothes from the middle of the country—someone who sold brushes door-to-door maybe—that trying-to-not-look-desperate kind of outfit—that kind of suit that wants to go unnoticed—a clumsily-folded handkerchief stuck in the breast pocket—yellowed. He was old—hard to tell how old. I imagined he was the type who collected insects or stamps—who lived in a single room—whose landlady hardly knew him—who—other than common courtesies—spoke to no one—who slept in a narrow bed and who had always slept alone—who didn't have a car—who maybe had a small pension from his life as a clerk in the county tax assessor's office—who preferred dim light to sun—who did not go to the beach—who disliked sand—who disliked pets—who never stole—who did not pray but who once lit a candle for someone in a church—who had never traveled much—who did not vote—who did not have a credit card—who did not drive—who received no mail—who did not have a phone—who was meticulous and clean—who wore only clothes he'd purchased long ago. The truth was different.

INSIDE OUT

Dr. Winker says our stories are just the clothes our identities put on to go out in public. I wear my sweaters inside out so people have something obviously odd to focus on and miss the rest.

VICE GRIP

That store on the corner—I call it *The Vice Grip*—I mean *The Vice Mart*—sells liquor—cigarettes—salty snacks—candy and lottery tickets—at least when the lottery was still operating they did—before someone figured out how to make every ticket a winner and a mob stormed and gutted the building—the building to the east of the old watch factory—the abandoned lottery building—at least that's what I've always called it. They don't have butter at *The*

Vice Mart. They have batteries. I bought some for my pocket flashlight once. The man behind the counter has the same response to every liquor purchase—*good choice* he says. I don't steal from *The Vice Mart* and I don't often buy things either. Mostly I walk up and down the aisles and look and make adjustments where things aren't tilted right. They're used to me. I don't outwear my welcome. I'm sort of positioning myself to get a job there maybe taking inventory or being some kind of aisle monitor.

WAKE-UP CALL

Getting my friend to get up in the morning is like trying to make flowers open in winter with a blow dryer. She says she wants to start a dog hauling business. You know—for people who need their dogs moved across town and don't want to drive them themselves. *I won't be doing the hauling myself* she says—as if it weren't obvious—*You can't make money working—it's all contracted out—I'm just here at home leveraging my idea.*

VISITOR

A man whose house had burned came to the door. It was one of those stories with everything in triplicate—insurance companies—contractors—bureaucrats—all crooks—all out to get him—all falling down on the job of making things right for him—a world all porous and crumbly with corruption and ill-will. What did he want—maundering on about all he'd tried to do and all the setbacks—a labyrinthine punch bag fest of struggle and dead ends—what did he want—he stood in the doorway eyes darting was he drunk or had he been drinking or drugging or was he made this way all slurry and inordinate and sliding all around like a car on ice—black ice you can't see right away—can't see at all sometimes—on and off the road—into the weeds and brush—a story like that you don't even want to follow—a hula hoop monologue with lots of effort put into keeping it going.

His buttons were those of a man with a wealthy past. Had he killed someone important and taken their coat? Had he found a corpse and stripped it clean? Had he pulled the coat from a cloak-room and scurried off mumbling about what was due him by right of some long forgotten slight? He kept having this closing motion with his hands as if he were completing something—concluding his point—arriving at the crux—but there was no point being made except the way a mudslide makes a point—*forgive me* he kept saying—trapped in the flypaper wing-beats of talking—*forgive me forgive me*—as if I could conjoin the body and the breath—as if I could mend his broken-as-bad-knees discourse—tie its all-in-pieces parts together—as if I were the Fate of Fastening.

NIGHT

In the night in the night that pulls the parts of the day apart and hurls them sideways inside the furnace of sleep the windows have no glass no frames no walls the windows are the windows the wind is when the wind has its hands full of daylight and who knows what—and who remembers ever buttoning anything in a dream—in the hurricane of night—where things that hold the world together are lost.

FAIRY TALE

In the fairy tale a girl walked by a river and in the rushes—reeds—sedge—found a cargo box wrapped tight in brown paper and twine. Inside was a tin of buttons that she thought might be magic but soon found were not. Even so—the buttons in all their beauty cast a spell across her life and she gathered more and more.

BUTTONS

I found buttons in the dust—in the debris—in the ruins—on streets under piles of crushed plaster—on thrown-away coats—

in the coatrooms of abandoned schools—under stacks of tossed fabric—littered across split floorboards. Many of the buttons were broken—snapped in half by blunt force or trudging boots—many were torn from now lost garments—still threaded through as if about to be sewn. I cleaned them with care—one and one and one—*because by ones is the world begun again* I think I read or overheard somewhere.

I found a kind of beauty when I swept the floor today—dust fine as sifted flour—lifting and spinning and shifting with the same almost-will as weather.

FITS AND STARTS

I think the store at one time sold fits and starts—at least that's what the lettering on the sidewall seemed to say. Maybe they'd have taken my used ones. Anyway it was abandoned now and the glass of the front window had a long crack that ran diagonally and caught the light so it shone the way some boundaries made of brokenness shine in your life. I went inside as the door was half off its hinges—just open enough for me to slide through sideways. It was dusty and dank and picked over in there but I rummaged my way through everything I could find—tabletops—drawers—cabinets—boxes set on the floor as if intended to be unpacked but left as they were when something violent happened in the street—a wreck—or a fight—or an explosion—so what was being done became like lit matches you have to put down—like that friendship that changed at your fingertips into something that was after you like lit matches are after you when you hold them—or that dream of being pursued I told you about where you had to throw everything down just to get away and that pull chain of things happening drew you farther and farther away and you never returned.

BLACK ICE

My father told a man—in conversation on a train—that he was an educator—that he offered quick classes on office skills—like *how to load a stapler—how to line-up a hole-punch—things that were hard to understand but people didn't want to ask coworkers for help—then advancing to things like the miracle of alphabetizing.* Black ice on a black asphalt road.

METEOR SHOWER

I saw something of my father's in a pawnshop—at a yard sale—on a bus that went to the sea. He's in pieces across the city—a scattering of remnants—a meteor shower.

Sometimes you wish the dates were worn off all the coins—because then they couldn't carry you back so suddenly—so starkly—then the years wouldn't be those stark single things stamped there in the lower right—the dime I found in the dust in that vacant lot—that year sealed off in its circle—brushed clean between my thumb and forefinger—the date so crisply struck—as if that year were indelible. That year is not indelible. That year is gone.

NEEDLES

I'm planning my trip to Needles—stashing and rationing—cash in the lining of my coat—shrink-wrapped food in a backpack. I don't want to starve right away you understand. The trip will go like this—there's a kind of bus that pretty much goes everywhere nobody else does. It leaves from the Square of Nothing once in a while and with little notice. You have to show up again and again and wait and wait. You'll be surprised how many people are going nowhere. The bus is old and immaculate like the driver. You have to pay extra for a window seat. You'll pay it. Interstates aren't taken. You go through town after town—each farther and farther apart. Everyone on the bus is out of words. It leaves the city's orbit like a moon thrown from a planet by an impact. The world back there is gone for everyone. This binds the silence.

ASPERGUM

Dr. Winker says my headaches come from *clenching in the night* but I know it's the Chiclets I can't stop chewing box after box and the mandible-lock I get so I started eating aspirin lots of aspirin until I discovered *Aspergum* which is basically Chiclets made of aspirin. I think people took them for toothaches before there was dentistry. You can get them all the time—they're not illegal. I rotate stores because I don't want to be noticed stealing and stealing them. I'm not an addict you know—just a bit of a habit maybe—the slightly tart candy shell—cherry or orange—the bitter hook of aspirin underneath. The acrid is always what addiction wants—the bitter heart of the habit-forming—you need that corrosive quality in the taste—or the needle—or the cigarette—or the heavy-bottomed shot glass cut like a set of inward-facing windows. The edge that addiction holds against your life—it's in that taste—that thing that at first you hate but then you crave.

SCISSOR DAY

One Scissor Day I burned the map I'd stolen. All that knowing where you are and what comes next—the burdens it brings.

I cross the *Dark River of Fall Bridge*—the blue bridge across the river that one of the streetcars crosses—and I watch the huge bulk cargo ships—hulls open—filling with grain pouring in and making gold clouds that drift like cannon smoke across the river above the glistening water.

FAVORITE COLOR

I think self-discipline is for people not fortunate enough to be born driven. I got those calf-lock leg cramps again last night—too much walking I guess.

Dr. Winker clicks his mechanical pencil—asks me to choose my favorite color from a stack of color-cards. I'm thinking *he must be desperate*. I point to blue—you know—something tranquil just to keep him off my back. You don't want to open the door to a room you don't want to enter.

Flare-red is my favorite color—on distant highways at dusk—no towns—no houses near—two lanes fraught with hazard—they made the thread of cellophane flare-red that fastens things closed you shouldn't open—don't open these things—you have been warned—it doesn't matter it doesn't stop you—those who rebuke you don't know a thing about that red how thin and fine it is how all things cut just so are red like that—like that cellophane thread that seals the Aspergum tight as cigarette packs—that little flare-red thread you pull around the top like that magic thread you tug to unravel the world.

GRASP

Sometimes you just want to find a way to grasp the light and hold it—I mean keep it—lift it out of its endless perpetual transit. Not some light you think about in physics—not some theoretical light—*this* light—*this light* in the room *right now.* Sometimes the sky at midday glistens as if glitter were flung from the highest buildings.

The dust in the air today was once the Kelso Building mostly I think—now mixed with other detonated buildings—with dust from the grain-ships. Once it looked over the river. One morning I'd walked those floors.

II

Midnight as a Second Language

LIGHT FELL

I remember walking with my father one time on a street in an old part of a city—in very early autumn and the freshness of the air—its lustrous clarity—still nearly blinds me even as I just recall it now. We were on our way to some breakfast of coffee and pastry or coffee and eggs and toast. Something was going to happen that day or I thought it was. I don't remember what. I just remember that moment of walking down that street—I think there were cobbles but maybe I made that up. I know sliced light fell like an unhinged wall across and through me.

THE PIX

The Pix theatre is deserted but they still show movies there. I go from time to time. The neon sign no longer works and the pink chipped paint is mostly worn away on the deco façade. The concession stand is permanently closed and the ticket booth is uninhabited. The seats smell mildly of mold but I don't mind. I think if you're going to make a private sense of the world you have to let go of the common world to do it. Like leaping from a swing as a child when the swing is at its apex. You have to apply yourself to a kind of flight.

The other day I saw a documentary at the Pix about a city made of cardboard and foil and broken tiles and broken glass and scraps of wood and wire—a city of twists and turns—constructed beneath stone archways—cement I mean—cement archways—room after open room and every detail right—that someone had built—maybe in the basement of a building or in an abandoned warehouse somewhere—and no one knew they were working on it or that it was there until one day that person disappeared and it was discovered and it was not like anything anyone had ever seen.

Sometimes a private sense of the world can be like walking on water from underneath—the time you fell through the ice and couldn't find the opening at first and you were walking on water with your fingertips from underneath and the water was frozen and white and below was black.

DRUNKEN WIND

Last night the wind worked its way through the city like a drunk clearing tabletops of glasses with his forearms in a bar fight.

Today the light between the buildings makes sundials of the streets.

MOTHS

Sometimes small moths in clusters find their way into my room. They weave and unweave in the air—they weave and unweave like Penelope's trickster shroud. I catch the moths—with care—one by one—sometimes three at once—in the air. I catch them with a wine glass and a postcard—standing on tiptoes—pivoting in a dance that they direct—and take them down to the doorway and let them out. They'll find each other I know or find their way back I think or wander the city and end up somewhere else.

You can't imagine all the things you can't control. You can't make the world small enough to make it certain. Smells of smoke intrude—smoke from burning leaves or smoke from firecrackers too far away to hear or lost in thought you just don't notice them.

THROWN TO THE GROUND

Have you ever known someone who died in an explosion—or someone blinded in a blast? Me neither. I saw some mining movies at the Pix—films of mountains being dynamited—someone always running for cover. Sometimes that someone didn't get away. I know what that's like—the mountain coming down—I can't remember everything I've thrown to the ground while running to get away.

BONFIRES

Sometimes from the roof I watch the bonfires in the streets—no one in attendance—empty streets. A time of fires untended in empty streets comes to every life I imagine.

HIDING THINGS

My mother was in the basement bleaching things. I was standing at the front window watching things disassemble across the street—a marriage splintered in shrill speeches—boxes packed and sealed with transparent tape—tables trundled down stairs—legs broken off by heedless hurried movers thinking of some life they could have lived if things had been less the same and more like something else. You've broken a thousand things that way—made things worse half-on-purpose—don't pretend you haven't. You hid something someone needed so you could be the hero when you found it. But then you waited too long and people started getting hysterical so you were afraid to find it because you knew they'd know you'd hid it so you just left it there and then finally when everyone had forgotten it you went and got it and took it out of the house and threw it away deep in a public garbage can where there weren't any cameras around—or the time you hid something dear to you where others wouldn't find it and got distracted and later forgot where you hid it and where was it and it was like being suddenly famished—the ferocity of looking for it—and then one day you stumbled onto it and it didn't mean that much to you by then.

Then there's that thing where you hide things from yourself—things you can't trust yourself to hold—that finger puppet play you put on for your ancient babysitter while she fell asleep with the lit cigarette in her hand. That's what Dr. Winker is all about—things you hide from yourself—where do you put them I wonder. Do you brick them up and forget—are there drawers in there stuffed with things to hide them under—are there gardens with little buildings—sheds—with buckets of tools or blocks of dried out sod. Are they really still really there—he doesn't know any of this—he just wants to dig them out—or have you do it actually because he doesn't really work. What he does I could pretty much do for myself I think—just keep talking and being interested and asking follow-up questions and see what happens. I can't remember who first sent me to Dr. Winker or how I found him or how long I've been seeing him. I asked him once but can't remember what he said and I don't want to ask him again because that's like the time you cheated to let someone else win.

WHERE TO START

No one knows where to start when you start them in the middle—and when you are waiting you are always starting in the middle—in the middle of waiting—starting there over and over—the way you come into life—right in the middle of this midstride universe—the way I started in the middle of being in this city somehow. Pressed against something blank you twist and turn inside yourself trying to connect who you are—what you've done—with some notion of yourself that sets things right.

SETTING THINGS RIGHT

I took a rich friend's dental retainer—the one her mother made her swear up and down she would not lose—and threw it in that small deep lake near my house—the one I used to walk around and watch change from season to season from green and fresh and wild to white and frozen and settled as that lawsuit between a firefighter's widow and the ladder maker. The ladder maker's wife became a widow too. She and the firefighter's widow became best friends because they both had a passion for quilting and their quilting motto was *if something's ugly you just haven't made it small enough.*

COOKIE TIN

I lifted a tin of Italian cookies from the discount store—pictured as elegant thin blond almond wafers—lightly sugared—the kind where when you take the lid off there's stiff embossed paper over the layered wafers and you have to peel it back and it makes that crumply stiff paper sound that makes you want the wafers even more. But then there was something else. The lid would just not come off. As if it were welded shut it wouldn't budge. And I tried that thing where you go around the rim underneath and try to pry it off in rotating stages and it still won't give so finally you force it.

DOUBLING

Did you ever wonder if someone might be pretending to be you—wandering the city—going about your life as if it were their own? That time the man with the monocle said when you entered his shop—the shop that sold miniatures—*you've been here before*—but you had never been there before in all your life. And you set it aside—unquestioned and unexplained—like all the fingernail type things I talked about earlier—not thinking how someone had pretended to be you.

MINIATURES

Some people like things in miniature—trains—porcelain dogs—glass cottage candy jars—things that look like real things but smaller. Maybe actual things aren't really the right size for everyone. Most of the things that sweep you away can't be made smaller—can't be made manageable—can't be right-sized for your hands or for your life. Maybe life in actual size isn't right for everyone.

Betrayals are never their actual size—serving suggestions on cereal boxes aren't their actual size you understand and things that are farther away aren't actually the size they seem to be. Maybe actual size things aren't right for everyone. Life's mostly actual size except in memory where things are larger or smaller than they were I think I've said. Some things aren't made to be their actual size—the way things were in that shop selling miniatures that time. The way the proprietor insisted you'd been there before.

Maybe you make your way around things like mercury does—the way my father made his way around the truth—so actual sizes don't hold your interest much. Words aren't the actual size of things they say—what is the actual size of the sea—of a wave—of the wind—of the stories you tell yourself that cut everything down to that size that you can manage. No one ever got blindsided by a miniature.

ATLAS

I found an atlas from in abandoned school. Water damage left some pages curled. Some countries were spotted with mold as if new cities had sprung from flooded lowlands. Some countries were yellowed as if by cigarette smoke blown across their borders. Sometimes I get my atlas out and retrace the train trips I took with my father—our travels all over the world.

SEARCHING FOR THE PAST

I have looked through the house. I have looked through the house for photographs—the drawers are bare except for clothes and undated documents—documents that say nothing—saved for no purpose. I have searched through the house for the past that any house has stored inside—that any house where people have lived holds onto—I have searched and there is less almost than you'd find in a motel.

WALKING INTO THE NIGHT

My father taught me midnight as a second language—its miles upon miles invented as we went—of things found in ourselves—the way we each make worlds of words within reach.

Sometimes we'd walk into the night—the great unpressurized emptiness of a city deserted by sleepers. Car hoods glistening under streetlights—shop windows with dimly lit displays—our steps on the pavement echoing—out to the boundless sea—the stars in their numbers thrown across the sky—shoes off—sand sticking to our feet—sitting on the seawall—talking in circular sentences or nothing said—huddled by the driftwood fire we'd built—sparks ascending and dying—blinking back smoke when the wind would shift—sometimes falling asleep on the cold sand—waking hurting and laughing—walking slowly and stiffly back to the house.

THE WITCH'S HOUSE

I get confused about where *the holder* lives—it's like some fairy tale of the house that's not in the same place over and over—the witch's house in the weed-tangled wood—that's here—then there—then nowhere to be found. Sometimes the streets look all alike—the houses too. How many strangers have you seen in your life? How many can you remember?

MOSQUITOS

My friend is the kind of person who thinks mosquitos only bite you where you need it. She won't kill anything. Even flies. She traps them in glasses and opens windows and lets them out. No surprise I rinse my glass whenever I drink at her place because I don't want to drink from a fly-glass even though she says it's good for my immune system and on sensing that I'm not reassured she blurts *no one ever died drinking from a fly-glass. As if dying were the only reason not to lip a fly-glass* I think maybe under my breath—and then she launches into some blame-you speech that laces longer than a knee-high riding boot and none of which can you even begin to remember like that twisty-road car trip your parents made you take through the mountains when you were woozy after gulping a bunch of little-kid motel hot-tub pee-water and eating a share-size bag of peanut M&M's and all you can remember is wanting it to end.

STREETS BRUSHED WITH GOLD

Sometimes inside my head is like a brushfire—a restless all-consuming commotion of smoke and crackling. Some mornings the streets look like they're brushed with gold—the way the light lifts upward from under the dust and makes it glisten. Some mornings the days that start that way seem workable. I'm not talking about how you manage things to turn out in a particular way—not workable like that—I'm saying you can see how you might fit into the day the way something fits into your hand when you lightly close your hand around it—the way the day starts open around you and closes slowly until no light gets in and the day is over.

TOURNIQUETS

My friend has this thing for tourniquets—something that tightens-off poisons—keeps them from entering the system—stops the heart from stopping cold. What can we use for a tourniquet is the question basically underlying everything.

THE HOLDER

I don't remember who this woman is—the woman who comes to the house—*the holder*. Remember when you had your wisdom teeth taken out and they put you under and you had the whole weird aftermath where your mouth was not your mouth and your cheeks had rocks from somewhere stuffed in them and you had this story about what had happened to you but you really remembered nothing? I have some versions of who this woman is but I can't be sure. I have some versions of all kinds of things that I'm not sure of. I can't ask her again who she is—I just can't. You know that person you've met at three parties and can't remember their name and you just can't ask them again and you can't pretend not to know them but you don't know them really and they always know your name and call you by it and you have to drive around the conversation avoiding having to say their name which soon they know you don't know and it was OK to ask them again at the second party because anyone can forget a name from a single meeting but not a third because now they know they mean nothing to you and you are self-involved and self-concerned and they don't interest you which they do not but this woman who comes to the house every other day or so is of interest to me and I know I've asked her maybe many times who she is and why she comes to the house but I can't remember any of it and I'm pretty sure she knows that I can't remember but I'm not absolutely sure so I just can't ask her again and now you understand why.

DEATH IN THE DOORWAY

Maybe you are solid as packed soil. Here the days evaporate like spills. Mostly movies featured at the Pix are black and white—

films from some other time when things were more clear-cut. Last night's movie was about a man standing in a doorway day after day and the man was death and no one noticed him standing there because he was plain as sand. Everyone was on their way to someplace else. The man in the doorway went nowhere.

SUBTITLES

Sometimes the films at the Pix are in other languages and the subtitles don't seem to match what's happening on the screen. Usually I can't read fast enough and I'm trying to go back and forth between the scenes and the dialogue if you know what I mean.

I had a friend who basically supplied subtitles to the lives of those she knew. Whatever you said she came back with what you really meant or a better way to say it or something like that and you knew that in her mind the subtitles to what you were saying were flashing on a screen and she was just reading them aloud to you. Did you ever have a friend like that where you started to wonder how you ever made sense of anything without them—how you ever made sense even to yourself—and then you realized that you didn't make sense to yourself and nothing made sense around you and you'd needed those subtitles all along but maybe she's not the person you'd have chosen to provide them if you'd had a choice. Anyway I made her some business cards that had her name and under it was *Subtitleist* and when I gave her the cards and explained what it meant she didn't give me subtitles to what I'd said she just got mad and left and took her subtitles with her and I didn't understand what the problem was because she wasn't there to explain it all to me. Anyway there was a whole film about something like that at the Pix the other evening. Something about a married couple who subtitled each other all the time. It ended badly. It was black and white. It had no subtitles. I wanted to see it again but they only showed it once.

SEMINAR

Enthusiasm is just a way of finding fault with others. That seminar *the holder* sent me to that showed me I was just a small shift of attitude away from being someone I'd admire—the one with that lady at the front of the room who cheered herself on like a house fire—wow you could be someone more dynamic and seaworthy and desirable and more hirable and more on-the-ball and more productive and pushy in a good way and just generally *more*—and that seminar leader with her siding of perma-perky grating against you like that time your little friend with the lazy eye from behind the counter at the family-owned sundry store made you a backscratcher out of old upholstery tacks and it was your birthday and you had to use it right then and there so you wouldn't hurt her feelings and why didn't your parents just keep a drawer in the fridge full of tetanus shots you wondered.

SALES ASSISTANT

I decided to try on being a sales assistant—a silent one so as not to be too pushy. My friend said she was behind me fifty percent. I'd go into stores and help people decide to buy things. It isn't hard—you move in—but not too close—you muster a warm smile—you look them up and down—you point—you gesture toward the item they'll purchase—you wink and nod—they see that you approve. They won't find this item again. It looks great on them. Sometimes I offer encouragement at the entrance to the dressing rooms. Sometimes I'm at-large and opportunistic. It helps sometimes to escort the customer to the checkout—just to cement them to that thing they're going to buy. Cementing like that is mostly what the job requires. I don't want you to get the idea that I'm intrusive. A good sales assistant is never intrusive.

You know about wanting things—I know you do—the impatience of it—the plans—the way desire is always making plans—the way desire stays with you no matter what you have—the way it never abandons you to the life you've got—hustles your steps up flights of stairs and down flights of stairs—stairs and stairs—climbing and descending—how you think there's an end to it—just on the stair above or the stair below. Take a step. Take another.

Some people just can't stand it if you show some initiative. A security person who looked like some vampire's fallen creature *removed me* from the department store—*with a warning*—just when I was closing in on a client.

AMBER

You don't know the shape of your life so it's hard to shape it—where to cut at the edges—where to cut through the center. I found the chunk of amber I'd lost—in my cousin's drawer when I was going through her things—and I knew she'd stolen it and I didn't know how to bring it up so I silently stole it back but then I had to hide it even though it was mine because at the time I thought my cousin mattered more to me than that chunk of amber and I wanted to somehow have them both even though now I knew how little I meant to my cousin.

COLD

You have to ask yourself what kind of coldness you are capable of—don't back off—you are capable of being cold. But how cold—this is what you must know about yourself—how far can you turn the heat down in your heart—cool—freezing—below freezing—zero—liquid nitrogen cold—I mean a metal-cracks-and-breaks kind of cold. You can say you can't know until that moment arrives when you must be cold but I say you know without doubt where you've needed to freeze things out—look—see what you've done—been willing to do—to freeze something out—but not something—someone.

Do you know what it's like to break a wooden yardstick over and over again—the pain—the splintering—the snapping—the pain in your hands—that kind of cold electrical heat—and each piece harder to make break than the one before? Dealing with dismantling goodness in your life is a task like that—a task like taking what measures and breaking it smaller and smaller until it is only inches—until it is parts of inches—until it measures nothing. You cannot conduct this work with your own bare hands—oh you can to a point—but the time will come when your hands don't have the strength to break it further—you must find pliers or vice-grips or vice-grips combined with hammers or something strong and steadfast to combine with your will to break and break and break.

MERCURY

I like to walk close to buildings. I like to be out of the way. I talk to myself incessantly—as if talk were the edge of something barely held. I stole some mercury from school because it was so beautiful and nothing in the world was like it and they'd named a planet after it but then I didn't know what to do with it because it was so dangerous and I couldn't keep it and I couldn't throw it away like that locket your grandmother gave you with a lock of her hair inside. And how many things can come back together on their own after shattering—not many I've noticed—that time I tried to epoxy my amber-thieving cousin's toe back on after running the push-mower over it and she wouldn't hold still and she wouldn't be quiet and she wouldn't be fixed and *why can't she just be like mercury and fix herself* I thought.

TRAINS

The train pulled into Arad Romania. The black market money-changers working the side-streets near the station turned out to be government agents and my father was nearly arrested and had to bribe them mightily to let him go and what if they hadn't and what if they'd charged him with bribery as well and he'd been carted off and I'd have ended up in the house of some colonel who'd used me for services and one night I'd snuck off and managed somehow to hide under a tarp on a produce truck and then found my way on a coal train through Bulgaria and into Turkey and finally in Edirne I slept on a bench in a park but only briefly and eventually I crossed into Greece and found my way down the coast and across the Aegean to Iraklion and found a Minoan shard in the dust of the ruins and ended up giving tours to British tourists and one fell in love with me and I did not love him but he was rich so I went with him back to London and we married against the wishes of his family and I had three children by him and we had a long and tolerable marriage in the country on a small ramshackle estate and of the three children one was by far my favorite and she asked me about her grandfather and I told her I had no idea where he was or what had happened to him but the last time I saw him he was under arrest and being led away.

WHOLE CLOTH HISTORY

Dr. W says I've made a whole cloth history. That sense of taint again is what I get—as if memories made whole cloth were a kind of lying—as if the generative and the false were not conjoined—as if the imagined and the retrieved were not twins torn from one another in storms or when you were learning right from left and trying to remember which hand was which even when if you closed your eyes they seemed the same—all sides—all things with things on either side are like this I think—learned or imagined or retrieved and with which hand one does not initially know and when it is learned it starts the dissevering of every unity of every whole cloth thing into this and that into one or the other into that relentless holding to account you think constitutes the substance of yourself the holding to account of everything arrayed in your path as either true or false of value or worthless or worse and I want you to think the way I do for once how your memory has more holes than the fossil record as if there's no room for the random as if memory were not the sea a continuous miraculous reshuffling of its billions and billions of things as if things have to be directed like traffic after a wreck where people have been killed.

THE BUTTON-CHOOSER

I followed her once—the button-chooser—I noticed her walking close to buildings in her gray flannel coat. Who do you think decides which buttons go on which garments? Have you ever thought of this? Have you ever thought of that person? How she rises in the morning—you know it must be a woman—and walks unnoticed to an office in a factory somewhere. The office is gray—one small window—looking out on a parking lot or a light well—but the button books are bright—page after colorful page. She turns them in silence. No one bothers her. The button-chooser's work is lonely and deliberate and pure. I knew her at once—all the way through—like light knows glass. Her eyes so keen and clear. Her buttons—their strange incongruent perfec- tion. It was dusk—night falling fast. I followed her to the long-vacated Eisler Building. She turned and went in. A light came on in a room above *Bon Voyage Travel*—which I think was a mortuary. After a little while the light went out. I waited. I watched. She left. I went in and up the stairs. The door to the room was not locked. The room was small with bookshelves lining the walls. I did not turn on the light. My pocket flashlight scanned the button books she'd taken and hidden when the button factory closed. I took them down and leafed through heavy page after heavy page—buttons the color of silver—the color of pewter—the color of brushed chrome—the color of raw iron—the color of blown ash—the bright color of bone—the brittle white of northern light—the gray of granite—the lustrous black of a polished stone—sea gray—sky gray—gray as the shimmering surfaces of water when the wind wavers and then accelerates—pistol black—tire black—a gray more muted than moss—white as lichen salted across a stone—deep gray ferns—gray and white as gull feathers—the almost black of a plum—the graphite gray of scuff marks on a white linoleum floor—white as polished plates set in the sun—flake-black—burnt gray—rust. I did not steal a single button from the button chooser's books. I put them back as they were—neatly stacked—sorted by color and type.

COOKIE TIN

I stole a tin of Italian wafer cookies—so beautiful—*on clearance—why*—I wondered—it turned out to be the lid—I think I told you—which you could not remove it was so welded shut—that thing that you find with some people where when you lift one side—pry it up—the other side closes down more tightly so you try to open that side and the opposite side tightens in a commensurate operation that manages to keep you busily at it while thwarting any progress—the tin was like that. The cookies too were not as good as they looked—too sturdy—like thickly starched craft paper—the bit of sprinkled sugar did not help but only served to remind you of the distance from where you were to what you'd imagined. Sugar is tricky like that—all things that are tried and miss the mark are tricky like that—a kind of psychic jujitsu ensues that takes the energy of expectation and turns it on itself to throw you skidding face down to the mat. The product was apparently designed to be purchased only once—like being alive—that maybe there were just enough unsuspecting souls around to keep the maker in business.

WHITE-OUT

Dr. Winker says that memory is just a rewrite—by excision—of your life. I almost called him *Dr. White-Out* after that. He says it's all still in there—everything that ever happened to you I think he means. I don't believe it—how can it all be in there—you know all the errant socks aren't in there—all the loose change—the crumbs—the paperclips—the words you couldn't come up with—the leaves on tree after tree cascading down piling up everywhere—all the light deflected from surface after surface—all the light—the uncountable hours that forced you through the funnel-neck of night—you know it's not all in there—and trusting memory to name what it's forgotten is like that teacher trusting the class to self-grade the biology test.

MYSTERY SHOPPER

I used to be a mystery shopper—or double as one. The whole idea is to make people be rude to you by being stupid. With the cast iron pot you ask if they can sell you just the lid because you lost yours. You ask if they can sell just one of the gloves because you lost the other. You ask if there is another branch of the store within walking distance where the service is better. You take out a notebook and start writing the ruder they get. You take out your notebook and start speaking to them in a completely different way—a way where they know at once that you are smart—that you are smarter than they are—and then they have that look of someone caught in quicksand without a stick to grab.

I still send my reports to the mystery shopping service and sometimes to the stores because at that seminar I was telling you about—the one *the holder* sent me to—*Instructor Perma-Perky* said that—in life—you can't just apply for things like jobs *you have to be those things* and then someone hires you to do them. So I'm being the best mystery shopper ever and when I've stacked it all up on their desks I'll apply and be hired to do it. You can't let other people set limits on your life with what they are willing to see you as you have to tell them what they're looking at and then they usually accept it for what you've told them so I understand.

THE PIX

I've thought about taking someone—maybe someone I found on the street who I thought could be my friend—to see a film at the Pix but what if she couldn't see it—what if—for her—the screen was mostly just shadowy and blank—what if her inside projector wasn't working—the one that takes what's on the screen and lets you see it in yourself. Then I'd have to try to explain what was going on which meant I'd be talking but that would probably be OK because maybe—other than ourselves—the Pix would be empty. I'd probably have to give up on the idea that she could ever be my friend because maybe what was happening at the movies wasn't her cup of tea—didn't matter to her—was like most of what doesn't matter to people as they march through their busy lives—just not really there—just not on the movie screen inside themselves. I don't know where you go to get your inside projector fixed. Dr. Winker wouldn't be able to help you—that's for sure. Anyway—I wasn't suggesting anything else to her.

I know you think there aren't really films at the Pix. There are.

CRAZY AND SANE

The difference between crazy and sane is simple. If you print your own private money in your basement you can't expect them to take it at The Vice Mart. Sane people know this. Crazy people don't. That's it.

WATCHING

My father didn't drive or carry cash—like some Royal Highness. He thought self-improvement was a matter of diminishing returns—like makeup. I never really knew what he did or where he worked. He changed jobs pretty often I think it was—sold things I think—or *doubled as a salesman* as he'd say. I knew my mother sometimes had to drive him to his job—dropped him off a block or two away and he'd walk the rest like some kid trying to look grown up by seeming to get to school on their own. She'd pick him up at the end of the day—bring him home where he'd collapse on the couch in the living room. At the dining table my mother would do books for clients or pay bills while my father slept. No sound at all in the house—except her soft fingers on the calculator keys. Sometimes she'd have a glass of wine. I'd listen for that sigh—deep as wells—when she'd finally relax. My mother did not complain. The wear showed up as a kind of flatness. The way flat things are always without complaint. The way complaint is always heavily contoured. She was not. I don't remember what I did except for watching them. I wasn't bored—the way when you're watching something stand—that you know cannot stand—you can't be bored.

MIDNIGHT

My father taught me midnight as a second language—the built and the imagined—shunted together in the switchyards of desire.

I know my father walked into the sea—sea of faces—sea of doorways—the locked-room mystery of memory.

TIDAL LOCK

In case you haven't already looked it up—*tidal lock* means not being able to see the other side of something. You can't see the other side of the moon because the moon is tidally locked with the earth in its orbit for example. Venus and earth are tidally locked. No one knows why. Things you can't turn from—things you can't shake—how the past turns its single face to you—how all you can't remember lies on its dark other side.

Expunging the false is not always an overnight thing—I mean making space for the truth. I can't collide with the past anymore in my house—in my empty house. Even if you seek a starker faith than belief allows—a bare-walls—empty-drawers—no-curtains-on-the-windows kind of faith—you will not be able to read right away by the light of all you've thrown into the fire.

KNIFE-THROWER

I wanted to be a knife-thrower—for someone to trust me with their life in that way—someone tied to a spinning board in a skimpy outfit and somewhat attractive—an enthusiast of sorts—a trusting enthusiast—enthusiastic about me that's the point—about my skill at throwing knives. You have to be enthusiastic about the things your life depends on—or at least seem to be. I wanted to save someone's life by not killing them—maybe with an audience—an audience who paid something to watch. Put someone in danger and see them through to the other side—a way to make a living by solving problems I create—sort of like a bureaucrat—but more immediate—more urgent—something more explicitly at stake. Knife throwing fills the bill in my opinion—saving people from dangers I put them in and being lauded for it.

A LADDER WITH ENDLESS RUNGS

Dr. Winker says my *problem* is *idiopathic*. It's kind of obvious what that sounds like. The house at the end of the road with no glass in the windows—no doors on the hinges—something is at stake every moment in a house like that. I don't expect you to understand.

A wind came up in my life—in the middle of something absolutely ordinary—some ordinary goings on—some inane happening—a wind came up that moved things on their axis—bent things—broke things. A wind came up from somewhere—so strong it was unlike any wind you've ever known it so shook the world—so shook my life that after it had passed my life was not left standing—my life was not my life.

Maybe I can be more precise and not get carried away and steady myself and tell you. I climb. It is like a ladder with endless rungs. I work my way higher. I pull myself up—steadily—over and over.

FAIRY TALE

My father encouraged me to make up my own fairy tales as a child and to tell them to myself. As if myth would build a world from all the stuff found lying around my life—my father's life—where I went on foot through brush and trash and shiny broken things.

A girl woke in a city with no memory of how she got there. She was alone—her father had disappeared and she looked for clues to find him. The city was not a city like any she'd ever seen. People hardly spoke and blond industrial dust descended steadily from demolished buildings. The girl lived in an almost empty house with a kind of caretaker who came by from time to time with food but who did not live there. The girl needed help from the gods but did not know how to get them to notice her. She began destroying everything she cared about—one thing at a time—on the anniversary of her father's disappearance. This had gone on for many years and this was why her house was almost empty. The gods—she determined—must balance the world—and her destruction of things she loved would have to be righted—righted by the return of the father she'd lost.

NAMES

I don't know the names of trees—or shrubs—well maybe a few—or flowers—well a few maybe. The things I know the names of aren't the things with names the way you'd think of them. Dr. Winker says the things I can't remember are like redacted briefings where the substantial stuff is gone and what's left is like a chimney standing in a vacant lot where a house once was—after a fire I think he means—except he says the house is still there somewhere and the work is to see that house that you can't see at all and maybe that's why the waiting room is empty.

Let's face it—Dr. Winker isn't what you'd call a together kind of doctor. He's unraveling even as he tries to make you ravel—like some diabolical tandem spooling thing where—while the one gathers the threads—the other forfeits them. At the end of every session he's a mess—fidgeting—blinking—mumbling. Not many professions someone like that can enter I imagine. It would have to be on the helping end of things.

The things I know the names of are things like *if you're brought up in the car business that's probably where you're going to end up.* And I know the name of that free-fall in yourself that you stumble into. I know that name by heart.

TOURNIQUETS

My friend said she was bitten by a spider—it was hiding in the base of her zucchini spiralizer—she said she picked the spiralizer up from beneath and the spider bit her on the finger and then it fell out on the counter and *reared up* she said *in that way that small angry things sometimes do*—rear up that is—and my friend tried not to panic and she told the spider not to be afraid and she put a glass over it and a card under it and took it out behind the

Castaways and let it go but then there was the matter of the bite and she told me she was not afraid to lose her hand but didn't want the venom to reach her heart so she got a sheet and tore it into strips and made a series of tourniquets like locks in a great canal—somewhere far south I think it is—and tightened them tighter and tighter until her fingers were turning purple and she wrote a note to me with her *last good hand* she said about what her last thoughts were—about to be that is—before she slipped into cardiac arrest—and her last thoughts were about me she wanted me to know—and she gave me the note when she saw me the following week.

TORN AWAY

I found a deserted theatre where they still show movies sometimes. I'll tell you about it later. Deserted places fascinate everyone—at least everyone even remotely interesting. What was the last thing done here by those for whom this place had been their lives you have to wonder. There must always be a story—a story that will likely never be retrieved—so you have to imagine how a place fell out of use and was abandoned. There must always have been a life—a life attached to this place—fastened to its fortunes—a life that stood abandoned and bereft when this place was gone—fell out of use—had to be left behind in the economies of utility and dust. You know how things are pulled from your hands sometimes that you've taken hold of—*wrenched* I think the word is—*wrenched from your hands* by converging circumstances—*by fate* it might be said—by necessities—unforeseen and cold as gears. Hands that are empty after such a thing—I don't think there's a word for hands like that—hands empty like that—hands having held what is now torn away. Every deserted place has hands like that in its history.

FREEZER BURN

Something I meant to tell you—my friend had a friend who became my sort of friend and she invited me to an all-day session to consider options for her future. She didn't make coffee. There wasn't a snack in the house except some pork rind dust in the bottom of a bag. She talked and talked—a monologue more laced with lies than a funeral speech. There were flipcharts and timelines. She wanted my help identifying *milestones* that she could *celebrate*. It all left a taste in my mouth like freezer burn or that time I left the ice cream out and it melted and then I put it back in the freezer but it would never be right again and why was that what had changed it was ice cream and after it melted it was still ice cream and when I put it back in the freezer well it had always lived in the freezer so why did it now get all icy and slicey and weird and that day was just like that meaning everything was the same all the ingredients and everything around them but it would never be right again just like that ice cream.

AFTERTHOUGHT

My friend's only version of thought is afterthought. After the spider catastrophe she had me buy a bite kit—with my own money you understand—to keep in her bedroom and she read the instructions which were mostly all the ways it couldn't help her so she told me to buy another kit for the car she doesn't have.

REPAIR KITS

You won't be surprised at what you can find in the glove compartments of abandoned cars—I mean cars with no one in them. What you want to find are flashlights and boxes of matches and unscented candles—what you want to find are maps and not repair records and not glasses repair kits with the screws so tiny you can't hold them between your fingers and you can't see anything anyway because you're holding your glasses to fix them needless to say and so many things in life are like that I think—things you have to do that make the thing you're trying to do impossible.

FREEZER BURN

In the middle of that friend of my friend's meeting with me about her future—after the *milestones* part—when I'd guessed she'd guessed *my* future wasn't worth a single flipchart sheet—I got up and went into her kitchen and started breaking things—anything I could get my hands on—thing after thing—cups—plates—saucers—glasses—things thrown against walls things thrown through windows—all the things you can break in a kitchen I broke.

GEOMETRY

Dr. W. put me though some *self-revealing* exercise where I had to pick my *geometric shape*. I chose the parallelogram. It wasn't hard—I know my lives run parallel to each other—I know I'm a single shape with sides that do not touch—will never touch no matter how far the days extend their lines. Dr. Winker smiled and winked when I made my choice. Of course you know it wasn't an affirmation but he acted as if it were—he's not alone—don't pretend you don't try to incorporate your idiosyncrasies into the regular habits of those around you. I wonder what Dr. Winker's self-revealing shape would be—maybe the candlestick or the wrench or the rope—maybe the living room or the library or the conservatory—maybe a shoot or a ladder—you don't have to live with the choices people hand you—the tests don't tell you that—the tests you're handed never tell you that.

THE PIX

On a side street in a somewhat seedy part of town where alleys proliferate lined with garbage cans and standing water pools from some hidden source—*is something broken somewhere underneath*—you know it is—it's the same with you—something underneath has cracked apart and on the surface something pools that people walk around—anyway there was a side door into a long abandoned theatre. You can't not know a place like this in yourself so I'm sure you can summon it to mind. I'm sure you can imagine it easily. And it was just as you would think. The gilded interior—the slight stench of mold—the disarray in the aisles between the seats—the heavy crimson curtains drawn back to reveal the screen—some seats up—some seats still down where someone saw a film and left and that was that.

The film began with neither the clatter of the projector nor the dust-filled beam from the projection room. The film began as if projected from behind the screen. Silent. Black and white—a short about a thread-pull kind of person—pulled through life behind a needle puncturing cloth. The folds in the fabric are tugged tight in such a life—pulled tight—you nearly cannot breathe. Walls close in in such a life—in a life like this you narrow your way—your carriage is a sideways eking out—a kind of penny-pinching kind of movement. She was this kind of person caught in a life like this—standing on corners trying to sort things out—looking into her empty hands—their splintered lightning of lines—their taut jumble of threads pulled tight across her palms.

GRAVITY WAVE

There's a hum that permeates the city—mostly at night—like something being held against a wheel—a soft whirring wheel—so something being buffed—not ground—something being polished maybe—polished to a sheen where something could see itself.

III

The Past is Patient

THE CARDBOARD CITY

I found the cardboard city in the basement of the Buckner Building—cement stairs leading down from a heavy metal door that rust had given voice—my pocket flashlight held out as I went. I had experienced this before—descending like this—into the dark and the farther down you go the colder it gets. No windows. No power. The whole underneath of the building closed and black. The city down there in the dark—under everything.

Transparent as tides the dead pull at your life. All that you have calculated has no weight in that cold space where they were. Maybe in that space you remember your life—the life that's yours now. Maybe now your life takes hold in that space the dead leave—in the houses they built and left empty—on the streets they paved—in the stonework—in the ironwork—in the work of their hands in thing after thing you never think about. Maybe your life takes hold—the way wildflowers and wild creatures take hold in empty spaces—spaces you take your eyes from—the way you take your eyes from where the dead have been. I shined my flashlight along those cardboard streets. I could not grasp the city in all its size. Room after cavernous room. Receding like memory into blackness. After a while I left.

FAIRY TALE

In the fairy tale the girl found her way into an abandoned house—a house the size of the sea it seemed—a place between worlds—

floorboards disarranged by weather and neglect. She wandered from room to room—mold and peeling wallpaper—dust and broken furniture—*how do things break themselves* she wondered aloud—*why do they never repair themselves*—she wandered for hours and hours—looked in drawers—looked in cupboards—looked under beds—found a trunk with a nightgown the color of nicotine—wanted to try it on but the stench stopped her—sat in the kitchen—at the table showered in plaster dust and dirt—listened—listened closely—what was that sound—no—nothing—she rose and went into the garden—its shape still evident in the overgrowth—all the work of hands and hands and hands stored in those stones laid across the ground in rows like calendared days. She dug her hands into the soil and lifted it to her face—the smell of everything original.

THE CARDBOARD CITY

I returned to the cardboard city that night with a backpack full of votive candles I'd taken from a church—and placed them around the city—in squares—on corners—in parks—on the flat roofs of industrial buildings by the river—and lit them. You didn't want to be there but you couldn't leave—like all the frigid terrors that will always be yours. I was afraid I'd run out of air down there. No windows. No ventilation—the candles consuming all that oxygen—hording it for themselves in exchange for light. How many things in my life had been like that—giving up what I needed in exchange for being able to see.

The city was built on sheets of plywood resting on sawhorses—the way model railroads used to be displayed. Some streets were water-stained where overhead pipes had dripped—some were bowed as if the earth had buckled in a quake. The cardboard city slowed me down—demanded that I stop—stop being fraught. I followed its streets with a staid deliberation—a patience for what was there—I mean a patience that let what was there show itself—not constantly stamping myself on everything—hungers—graspings—explanations—thirsts.

When you let something stand as it is you can stand as you are in front of it. The cardboard city stood that way with me—there in that basement—under stained cement and twisted rebar—in the uneven candlelight. I rubbed the dust from the cardboard building fronts—I rubbed the dust from the street signs the way you'd rub dirt from a dime between your fingers. Some streets had names that I could almost read. Some buildings had numbers.

RAINBOW BLADES

The girl was never at home in the abandoned house she'd found.

Memory marks things—almost randomly—the way iron leaves a stain—the way leaves leave stains on concrete of their outlines.

Once I asked my father if he ever tired of not being a single person—*whatever do you mean?* he said—with a distance in his voice like someone you're looking for in a huge house who's only sort of wanting to be found.

Those times you put your fingers in the whirring rainbow blades of the push-mower because they were beautiful and the harm they held was well hidden.

He was a debt-collector—or worked in a small-country consulate as a clerk. My father made his living on the phone or something like that—or behind a counter—or behind some desk somewhere—something along those lines—debt collector—car salesman—some kind of thief-inside-the-law—some kind of livelihood that doesn't make actual things I think it was. All your life you work and there is nothing produced that you can rest a cup or elbow on—nothing you can pour water into—nothing you can sit on or sip from or hold. He went from thing to thing—selling this—selling that—all with an alacrity that dazzled.

THE WOMAN WHO DIDN'T KNOW HER HUSBAND

I remember the story of the woman who came home to a man she almost recognized who claimed to be her husband and the thing was he knew her absolutely and their whole history and all the details of her husband's life and her history and the details of the life they'd shared together but it wasn't her husband she kept telling herself but he wouldn't leave and her friends were confused about exactly what was her problem and then she started to doubt herself and started looking for pictures and letters and evidence and nothing was turning up because it had all been removed she decided so she had a stark choice to either adopt this man as her husband or leave in the night with almost nothing and try to find her way on her own or maybe find her real husband somewhere someday.

Something like that happened in our house one afternoon when I came home from school and my mother was claiming not to know my father. She was pacing the living room floor—going back and forth—yelling—*I don't recognize you—You're not the man I married*—and she turned to me and said—*This is not the man I married— do you understand?* I did not answer. I went to my room and I closed the door.

RAT

There was a rat in my house today. Lovely—bright—afraid and bold. I have this window fan—there's a plug beneath the window—and I plug it in and put it in the window when it's hot. When it gets cool I take it out of the window and rest it—still plugged in—against the wall below the window. The rat was running all over the place and I was chasing it with a bowl to put on top of it and trap it and then get something to slide underneath so I could carry the inverted bowl outside and let the rat go but there was no chance of catching the rat. It would curl up in corners briefly but I couldn't get the bowl to fit the corner and it would scurry and jump and it was so fast and it was silky and mocha and its bright black eyes were alert and almost human in their focus—in the way you could see the thinking happening behind them—and that thinking was of one thing only—survival. The rat ran under the stove and up the wall behind it where I couldn't reach it without moving the stove which I could not do. I waited in bed and—finally—the rat dropped down from its hiding spot and to my surprise walked into the bedroom—right across the middle of the floor—*aren't rats supposed to run along the edges of rooms where they will not be seen*—anyway I shut the bedroom door and pushed a shirt under it so no way out and then I pursued the rat again but no way was I going to get that bowl over it. It settled in the space between the fan and the wall. I was on my knees looking into its eyes. It was so calm—waiting for my next move—knowing it had a way out behind and in front of it. In a moment I slammed the fan into it—trapping it between the fan and the wall and crushing it slowly and coldly and determinedly. It let out a single last sharp squeak—and it was honestly the last sound of everything—shrill and hollow and final—and nowhere to go—and nothing next. I pressed harder—harder still. It was dead. And then it was like some spell had broken—some glove of icy indifference had shattered that had sheathed me during this—as if I'd been some other earlier thing—some almost human thing that had to have the rat dead and no remorse—and when it lifted—the tearing apart of every tender thing inside myself ensued—and I had nowhere to hide from it and nothing I could do would make it stop.

WALLS MOVING IN

I guess we all don't know ourselves sometimes. In winter sometimes when ice is on everything—that clarity that pulls you out of your life and you are standing there—as if something new were going to happen or—more plainly—that the past was completely absent in the single pure chill of that moment. I don't know what it's like for you—wandering the landscape of your life—even if that landscape is an apartment or a small store where you sit at the back with the owner and tell the same stories over and over—or pressed from all sides by some cramped marriage or almost marriage—*how many walls moving in can there be* you wonder sometimes I bet—there are no end to the walls moving in—to the confinement that comes from years of compromise—you might think on a morning like this—when all is cold and clear—that you could just throw the whole thing over and there is a power that surges in you that says it might be true but this wanes quickly and all the practical things flurry into your face and you know that you will not untrack your life—that you will keep to it and it will pay those shallow conditional dividends that it doles out in stingy sequences timed perfectly for moments just like this.

THE CARDBOARD CITY

Sometimes I'd sit for hours in front of the cardboard city or walk around it—room to room to room—following its streets with my flashlight or watching the flame-shadows waver or withdraw or widen on its walls. It took me a while to realize that the cardboard city was *this* city. Everything so changed. Slowly I started to tell myself the truth. As if the truth were a replica of the world. As if the cardboard city could stand in for memory.

THE WITCH'S HOUSE

In the fairy tale you do not go into the witch's house for any reason. You are not tempted to enter by being cold—by candy—by curiosity. You know if you enter that house you will not come out. You will never be found. Your hair will be braided for twine. Your bones will be ground for bread.

MIDNIGHT

My father taught me midnight as a second language—not because he meant to—but because I had to learn it to be with him. Like the time my amber-thieving cousin with the missing toe taught me how to swim by throwing me in a pond with my hands tied tight behind my back but with my father no one was going to happen along to save me.

TRACKS

Sometimes I see the railroad shavings glinting in the air—next to the tracks—swept up and spun around in the train's passing—a kind of metallic dust—if fireflies were pin points—maybe like that. I think if you breathe them in you will be restless all your life. I know how to hold my breath—how to walk steadily away—at an angle—you know these can't be learned all at once—maneuvers like these—you know the glistening shavings are only a chance to practice—to hone.

FOLLOWING THE HOLDER

The skills of disappearing—hard and unforthcoming—cannot be acquired quickly—that invisible space where you stand when you steal things—that angle where window-light can't catch you. You must learn to stand at that sideways angle just so—so that you are thinned—so that you are nearly window-thin.

I followed *the holder* in that sideways steal-things space of not being seen. I did not rush things. She was a woman of routine. I followed her in stages—dropping back—picking her up the next day at the same spot. I followed her to her house. I was across the street—in an alley behind some garbage cans—squatting slightly. I wanted to see her go in. She did not go in. She came across the street and confronted me. *You could have just asked me where I live—she said. You have before. I've told you before. I don't trust you in my house—the way you break things. I've told you before. Show me you can be trusted not to break things then we can talk. If I find you've been back here it's over—no more place to live—no more food in the fridge—it's over do you hear me—if you come back here you're on your own—no more spare change left on the table—nothing—if you come back here again you figure it out—you figure it out on your own.*

I hated her like someone strip-searched hates hands.

At home—as always—I ate by myself at the kitchen table with its hollow aluminum legs and once-white Formica top. Canned ravioli or something like that. Some kind of salad from a sealed plastic pouch—mostly shredded carrots and browned Romaine. Dressing like white spittle. Something trying to be bread. Water from the tap.

REVENGE

Revenge is something you learn not to waste. You don't middle-school squander it with overuse like swearwords or like that Little Miss Planet Perfect—pitiless and sharp as a popcorn husk—slicing her way to the top. No. You must wait. You must learn to appreciate how precious vengeance is. You must wait until that life-defining opportunity to get even arrives as last. You must hold it back like that Rottweiler that neighbor couldn't quite restrain without leaning fully back—that time it tore loose and mauled the lady across the street and she wasn't ever really right again and that neighbor fled to another state to avoid the suit but the lady had some thugs her ex-husband knew track that neighbor down and what happened to him was never spoken of but everyone knew.

In the cardboard city that afternoon I wanted to mark *the holder*'s house. I marked it with a hammer—beat it flat—beat it until the plywood beneath it split—ruptured—broke—beat it more—that thing where you just can't stop—you just can't hold yourself back

—that thing where rage carries on next to you and you are blinded and stunned and the self that rage has pulled into its hands like that hammer is thoughtless and heedless and can't be stopped and *go ahead* you say—*don't stop—don't ever stop*.

NEVER

You have never been to the city where I live. But where you live may have this city salted among its streets—city of tinsel-wealth—city of those fallen fitfully—of those fallen silently—streets of polished silver—streets abandoned—broken-to-pieces streets—cars polished—cars wrecked—lives suspended—lives propelled—lives gone under waves of seas unseen by those not drowning.

We've never met but maybe I remind you of someone you have known. Maybe I'm scattered among your friends and acquaintances—troubles with the truth—restlessness—search without ceasing—an aversion to sports and small dogs.

TURNING AND TURNING

I think Dr. Winker thinks he's a specialist—*dirty pain* and *flying debris* I think it is. He leans slightly toward me like the little helper-man in the sandpaper aisle at the hardware store—the one who builds his own fences and knows you can't. I think I may be Dr. Winker's only patient. The brochure I made without asking—that took me hours with cardstock and glue and pictures cut from my favorite magazines and ink made with vegetable soot—remains on the little table in the waiting room month after month. I'm not sure Dr. Winker is even a doctor. He always looks more comfortable with himself than you are with him. That's his *therapeutic lever* I think he thinks. Not that he looks all that comfortable with himself—but he's not like a being-bit pencil like you are—little chipped-paint teeth-marks all over you. Talk is like turning and turning—that green plastic see-through pencil-sharpener you used to have—the one you kept losing in second grade—that time you tried to dislodge the little razorblade to do harm to the child at the desk next to yours because he kept picking his nose and eating it. *Earwax tastes even worse* is what he said when you flashed your best disgust-face. You can't not wish you'd been born to a better species.

MOSQUITO

Being at my friend's is like being a mosquito on a camping trip—every time you eat someone's trying to kill you. From her freezer she took a zip-lock-bag of desiccated waste-meat with which she proposed to make soup for an early supper by adding water and more water and salt and lettuce and then boiling and boiling. She said the soup would go well with the cinnamon toast end-pieces she'd found I think in a breadbox she'd bought as a *collectable* at a yard sale and she asked if I'd set the table. I think the idea was next time—maybe even every time—I'd cook.

DEATH IN THE DOORWAY

In the movie at the Pix about death standing in the doorway—death doesn't pursue people—pick them out—tap them on the shoulder—carry them off. People find their way to death—in that doorway—in the course of their unremarkable days—and the earth closes over them like a hand grasping something long sought.

I first noticed the man in the doorway on an ordinary afternoon of hustle and bustle and shopping bags and scuffing shoes and stoplights and the broken blocks of light-and-shadow thrown down from tall buildings. I noticed him in that doorway—I saw him—though he was nondescript I think I told you. He was standing—stock-still—no shifting of weight from foot to foot—no glancing back and forth—the way ghosts stand I think—an empty standing like that.

You know the way you walk the edge of something—a conversation you don't really want to have—a spray of broken glass on the kitchen floor before you start to sweep it up. I go from place to place—from thought to thought—looking for an edge like that to step across—into the broken heart of something—even something bitter as batteries—even something acrid as crushed ants.

If you live in the curse of little crooked things—you can still turn your life just slightly sideways—if you know how to narrow yourself—make yourself thin—thin as a ticket—you can slip through a crack in the cardboard-staple-gun world.

I came out of hiding. I crossed the street. I whispered to the man in the doorway—*Are you death?* He responded—*Notice what's missing*. I gave him a button that shone like amber. That was it. I turned and walked away. The next day he was gone.

PUTTING THINGS RIGHT

Sometimes I try to put things right and it just can't work. When gravity wakes in a bad mood and everything just hits the floor—or that dream I had of trying to fix that thing I couldn't hold or trying to put teeth back that time I played Frisbee-plate with my cousin and made her catch first.

CATS THAT DISAPPEAR

There was a lot of fidgety vomiting at my elementary school. Mostly involving curtly corrected cursive and corn. I'd cooked dinner at my friend's and her tuxedo cat—*Kitty Little Cheese Strings* I think she called it or *Typo* or *Tingles* or *Lumber Skunk*—something like that—threw up on the dining room floor while I was serving. *At least he could have waited until after dinner* I said. She shrugged and said *I usually eat earlier*. So it was my fault—so I went to the door and opened it as if I might just leave—and the cat got out—and found its way out of The Castaways—and was lost and never found and that was my fault too apparently.

THE GIRL WHO FELL THROUGH THE ICE

I misunderstood everything. That time so many winters ago when the junior high school figure skater fell through the ice alone on the not quite frozen lake at the edge of town because she had a passion and wanted to get ahead of all the others and I thought she was still alive down there somehow having a terrifying adventure that she learned to be at home with and I swear I could hear her winter after winter tapping from under the ice. *You are not alive underneath in the frozen water* I came to understand when the teachers thought my self-esteem needed a boost and they assigned me to announce the school assembly and I got lost in the intervals and after the pledge and a little song from a little singing group I just dismissed everyone and they all ran out of the auditorium laughing and the students waiting to present just stood around bewildered behind the curtain and the teachers had to go gather everyone back but a few got away of course because you can't gather everything back that gets away and I was still standing there on the stage behind the podium and I knew right then and for sure that you are not alive in the frozen water.

TRAINS

The last time I saw my father was on a train leaving Barcelona—his back to me as he hurried down the aisle between the seats toward the exit.

THE INTERVALS

Sometimes I get lost in the intervals—those moments of being airborne between things that happen and things that are supposed to happen next—a hydroplaning car slamming a concrete median. Maybe you've forgotten that the intervals exist—the way you ignore the stretch of road between two towns—lost in your thoughts—lost in your plans for what will happen when you arrive. The thousand threads I asked you to think about earlier—or the finding no threads at all that I didn't mention. Some people spend their entire lives in the intervals—sitting on sidewalks—muttering to themselves—being avoided by everyone—not able to track—not able to pick up the ball—pull their weight—carry a conversation—make things happen. Some people are lost in the intervals all their lives—between jobs—between marriages—between channels on the radio where voices and songs and ads overlap and drown each other out. You may be a person like this yourself for all I know. Or maybe you've loved someone like this—maybe more than one.

THE PIX

I can't see into the corners of the Pix. Sometimes voices talk above the movies—sometimes there's the shuffling of feet or muted laughter or whispering. You can't ask people to be silent in a theatre that's abandoned. Often fear's edge—like the smell of mold but sharper—is right behind me in the theatre—and I have to speak to myself very slowly and deliberately and calmly the way you would speak to someone with a knife at your throat the way you would count on a kind of softness to save you—to save your life when you could not save it yourself—someone getting closer then withdrawing—the biting chill of their presence holding you frozen—something on the screen you couldn't turn from—something you needed to know so you couldn't leave.

CHOICES COMPOUND

The sea is an old story of ships—horizons—cataracts—a world where falling forms the only walls. A woman leaps from a bridge—so many times she'd veered from that narrow road in the rotary of her thoughts—now choices compound in the quickening space of the leap—in the interval without end—in the air as it brushes her face. The fates wait in motion—curled in readiness—like downward crushing waves. The skater who fell through the ice—the girl that everyone envied.

SECRET ROOM

I didn't tell Dr. Winker about the Pix. You can't tell people things you know they won't understand and then be mad when they don't understand them. You have to keep them back like children from a bonfire.

The Pix was like a bonfire in my life. I couldn't tell if I'd set it or not and I couldn't put it out—but mostly it was more like the secret room a child has in her house that she makes under the stairs or in a closet or in the attic—a place that's unused or full of unused things or things from the past—the past of other people some of whom she has never known and will never know because they are gone but their things are still here but unused or mostly forgotten—a place like that but not a place so entirely filled with things that there's no room to make a space—a space for the things *of* the child's life that mostly aren't of use *in* the child's life—the life that parents and other kids and circumstances make—the life to which mostly the child does not conform so she needs a secret place for her life to remain itself when it's out of step—which is most of the time—like the out of step things in these mostly forgotten parts of the house that stand against the engines that run the world—the engines of acquisition—and she needs a place to breathe and that place is there under the stairs or up some flights of stairs or something like that and the Pix was that place for me except for the fear.

PRETENDING TO BE BLIND

Everything finds a way to go sideways. You know this. Some force in the world unseen but ever-present pushes at angles against the fronts and backs of things in motion until they start to spin—until they yield and all that forward momentum is now harnessed to a skid—a flipping-over—a roll—a disintegration.

That time when you pretended to be blind so the kids at your new school—at the birthday party—the kids at the party—would feel sorry for you and look out for you. Or that time you pretended to be blind at that amusement park near your house—blind and lost and not quite willing to tell people who you were. You had to wear a small blond cropped wig so no one would know you—so you wouldn't be recognized—and some really really dark glasses. Anyway you wanted some people to want to help you. Don't pretend to me that you didn't do this. Don't pretend you haven't pretended to be blind—to not see what's in front of you—right there—and wanting sympathy for not being able to see it. The problem was you didn't know how to be blind—you didn't know there was something to know about being blind—the same way there's something to know about being able to see—and then people saw that you didn't know how to be blind—that you weren't blind at all—and then all that fury came out—that righteous justice kind of fury—and they were throwing snow cones at you and pushing cotton candy into your hair—which was OK because it was just a wig—and cursing you for not being really blind. How many times in your life has this happened to you? Stop pretending you've never done this kind of thing—not this thing exactly maybe—this pretending to be blind—but something really just like it—pretending to be something you're not to get something you want from someone who wouldn't give it to you if they knew who you really were.

FROZEN

The woman who leapt from the bridge—the one I was telling you about—for those she left—the torn fabric of that day is frozen—is a freezing—so nothing moves in it or near it—how it holds its frozen shape—that day I mean—stands in their lives but is not alive—cannot take a step or speak—cannot leave or be left—can never fit—can never be thrown out.

By what hand has the tearing entered—the taking hold—the ripping—by what hidden secretive hand has the tearing been engineered—the very closest hand that held the comb with which she parted her hair—the very hand with which she washed her face—tied her shoes—raised a glass of water to her lips—by that hand alone did the tearing enter with all its tugging force to pull her apart.

I lie awake in the dark—struggling to free myself from my thoughts—like someone trying to pull their wrists out of tied-tight ropes. In rail yards boxcars couple and decouple—slam—push—pull—in midnight's second language you can hear them—always sounding closer than they are.

LIGHTING FIRES

Did you ever can't-stand someone so much that you couldn't even tell them how much you couldn't stand them because then they'd want to know why you couldn't stand them and then you'd have to be around them over and over explaining everything you couldn't stand about them and putting up with them having to make it right so you could stand them even though you knew that was never going to happen because when someone you can't stand tries to make you like them well you just want to bludgeon them don't you.

I don't know how to be mad at my friend for being the person I always knew she was. She performs a kind of effortless psycho-ventriloquism where my own worst thoughts about myself come magically out of her mouth. Have you ever noticed how with some people you're trying to stomp out fires while they're always lighting new ones? My friend has a thing for setting fires like that—always another combustible thing alight in her life—always someone else's job to put it out. Maybe you've had a friend like that or maybe many. Maybe some people make problems and other people solve them in a kind of perpetual motion like that black white sun-driven whirligig in the sealed glass bulb that people used to put on their desks at the office or on their windowsills. Never get between someone and the trauma they've fastened to. I'd wanted to be a knife-thrower I think I told you. At least when you're stomping out other people's fires you're not thinking about yourself.

BAILING WITH BARE HANDS

It's always best to break things you have plenty of.

If things get broken at your feet you simply have to step around the shards—the way your reassuring words—empty as inside-out envelopes—step around the shattered sentences of that not quite casual acquaintance who's lost their child in a crash and you're trying to remember what you were looking for in that aisle of the store when they stopped you and now you're looking for that *get it off your plate* platitude that keeps things moving on the surface before you can actually step away and get on with your life.

What's the purpose of people talking to each other anyway? No one even asks. Things that really matter—matter to you—I mean the water that's coming in to drown you—people get impatient with things like that—no one wants to be at sea with you in that crowded little boat you're bailing with bare hands.

WHERE MUSIC COMES INTO BEING

I was trying to remind myself to notice what was missing—to remember to ask myself again and again to notice. Everything here of one piece—inside-out—outside-in. You just keep going in that face-value move-forward make-it-work-somehow kind of way. At first you don't trust yourself to stop—you don't trust yourself to stop and really see.

You stand in the intervals like a child stood in a corner facing a wall—a child who has daydreamed or fallen asleep—facing the wall as a kind of punishment—to be turned away and put against something blank. Maybe in that corner you can hear the weather—above the hushed chatter of the good children—the stay-in-their-chairs children—the children still free to stay in their chairs. Maybe above these children you hear the wind through a crack in the window next to you—another interval where music comes into being. You listen. You listen as others aren't. You learn—when you listen in this way—in this standing in a corner kind of way—that the sound of the wind finds you—that the way the others do not hear is a walling away of their being alive.

INUNDATION ZONE

At the outskirts something shatters. It reminds me of when I filled my mother's best thin crystal vase with water and put it in the freezer and how was I going to get all that shattered glass out of that freezer like how am I going to get that article out of my head that I read about the inundation zone along the coast that brings to mind when I rolled my back window down while my parents were taking the car through the carwash and it all just reminds you how we each live in our own inundation zone and whatever swamps your life you're always knee deep slogging through whatever it is like slogging through that speech that perfect person delivered about how you were doing everything all wrong and you had to listen and pay attention and appear to be learning something and how do you get rid of it like that time I had to eat creamed corn at the cafeteria and it was mostly cold because the power had gone out and I couldn't eat it anyway because it looked like what the neighbor kid threw up when I spun him harder and harder on the run-around carousel at the park so when my almost enemy sitting next to me wasn't looking I poured that corn in her backpack and then just flipped the flap and picked up my tray and moved to another table because that's how it works in the inundation zone—you always have to find a way to offload what's drowning you.

GHOST

My friend says a ghost came in the night and switched her eyes—*my right eye is lighter and now it's on my left* she said *and now I see everything differently—like a left handed person picks things up the opposite way—and I can't switch them back and I keep lying down and shutting my eyes and waiting for the ghost to switch them back but the ghost does not come back to switch them back to put the world back the way it was. Most people think their eyes are just alike because they've never looked at them really—my eyes were no more just alike than my hands—now how will I switch them back and right the world?* She puts her face to my face—*Do you see?*

PUTTING THE BUILDINGS BACK

At first it wasn't easy to match the city's vacant lots with the cardboard city's buildings—but eventually I managed. I cut the cardboard foundations—carefully this time—with an x-acto knife I'd taken from that art store I told you about and I lifted the buildings from the tables and carried them up the stairs. I went into the night—under moonlight—or with my flashlight—the streets empty—brought the cardboard buildings out—went to the vacant lots—put the buildings back where they had been. One-at-a-time. Night after night.

WALL OF THE LOST

The life of the missing is the part of your life that you cannot see as yours but also cannot abandon as someone else's. The Office of the Lost is now just a wall—the west wall—facing the Square of Nothing—of the building where The Office of the Lost used to be before it closed. No one remembers exactly when that was but it's been a while. People used to post notes—sometimes photographs—sometimes articles featuring some person unaccounted for—featuring what they did—who they were. At first there were some flowers in fluted glass vases and some plastic flowers for people who wanted more permanence and even some balloons—you know the metallic ones—for people who wanted to promote a kind of buoyancy. The wall was like pages of yearbooks populated with those who'd had a future but now didn't. Expectancy was always in the faces—the eyes especially—that look of something up ahead—even if that something was unknown—that sense of looking for it. That look is absent now from the eyes of those on streets and streetcars. That look has been replaced by a kind of wall—a wall of the lost.

PUTTING THE BUILDINGS BACK

In the vast vacant lots the cardboard buildings were nearly indiscernible. They were there nonetheless.

LOCKED-ROOM MYSTERY

A locked-room mystery was playing at the Pix. A locked-room mystery like madness. How did the killer enter—maybe through childhood—prying fingers pressing pliant clay—maybe wiring frayed from the start—something in the walls—gnawing the wires all along. How did the killer get away—maybe trapdoors and ladders—maybe ropes to the ground through self-closing windows—maybe that trick where air drinks a glass of water. Maybe the killer stayed—standing in a corner—narrow as knives. Maybe it stands there still—almost right next to you—no person after all—narrow as knives—no person at all.

Speak to it—as you would speak into insulation—press close—breathe the splintery glassy slivers in—something in the walls from the start—you are mute as caulk—speak to it—your words are white as drywall dust—beaded—sliding down—bend further bend closer—its ears where are its ears—your words are drywall dust on drywall white on white—press harder—write the name—the plea—the name—write it plainly white on white—the bleached crosshatched characters sliding down—its eyes where are its eyes?

INUNDATION ZONE

I looked for you and looked and looked and looked—a longing restless as boiling. *We're up ahead of us* you'd said. I don't know how things are made so narrow. You live with a circumstance that makes no sense to you. You have to make do with it. A woman is walking hurriedly down the street—crying. Not an insane person—an ordinary person—trying to out-walk the inundation zone inside her.

CENTERLINE

Dr. Winker is my therapist. He lives in the Pharaoh Building—or at least he's there every time I go. I almost called him *Dr. Centerline* because he says I have to find my centerline and stay to one side of it.

Maybe the wildflowers I remember from Death Valley could be my centerline—maybe the clouds in their transits could work like that—maybe the ins and outs of a locked-room mystery—like the centerline I crossed in my collision with being alive.

Dr. W wants me to be more practical.

I don't like peppermint stick ice cream—or people who do. People who like that kind of thing are the kind of people who make their own Christmas ornaments with felt—toothpicks—and white edible glue. People like that want their children to be true and strong and buoyant and they raise them in a succession of celebratory corrals. Their homes smell of scented candles and they get lots of cards in the mail because they send lots of them and people feel obliged to reciprocate. Do not cross these people. *Have some ice cream* they say—and you always know what kind it's going to be.

Maybe I could center my life on the tax code or golf like some people used to do.

Who drew the centerline anyway—you can't really know—maybe you drew it yourself as you went along—maybe it was an accident of birth—maybe it was gifted from the gods. Maybe your centerline is a broken line. Most are you know. Maybe *Dr. Broken-Centerline* can help. Probably not.

PREDATOR

I listen for my father's voice on crowded streets—in stores—in restaurants. The voices move in and out like cars among themselves. The voices move in and out like lacing shoes. He won't come out of hiding. I'm a predator now. He passes through street after street—he's lost my number my address my name the past the entire past—he sleeps on a train going north to the edge of some sea—through forests and meadows forests and flowers wildflowers and grasslands grasslands and tundra he sleeps on a boat moving north threading ice.

POOL-EAR

It's hard to feel sorry for someone you really don't like. My friend has *pool-ea*r again even though she never goes near water—*It's all echoey in there* she says—tilting her head and sort of shaking it—trying to get the water out—*maybe I should wear that nose-clip I had you buy for me—wear it all the time.* She doesn't remember where the nose-clip is. It's up to me to find it somewhere in the Armageddon of her apartment or go out and get her a new one.

BEST DAY OF MY LIFE

Everyone's had a best day of their life. For me it was outside of Edirne Turkey when I was teaching myself to drive with that rickety rental car we'd borrowed in Bulgaria and just kept and after we crossed the border it got a little wrecked and we had to hitchhike and some Turkish farmer picked us up but didn't have room in his truck so we sat in the flatbed trailer he was pulling and it was bumpy and jarring as we rode roughshod over rocks and washboard ruts and my father was trying to open a flat box of cigarettes he'd picked up at the border and they began to pop out of the box like popcorn kernels exploding in a hopper and he was grabbing for them in the air and we were bouncing along and laughing and laughing so hard we were hurting and rolling around in the flatbed of the trailer with straw and dirt and dust in our hair and crushing the cigarettes at least the ones still in the trailer like that German Shepard who lived down the street from us and had a litter of puppies and rolled on them and they died one after the other and their eyes were sealed slits and their tongues were poking out and the kids couldn't pull themselves away and the mother-dog was indifferent as an anvil—or like the over-mothered kids across the street the kids cornered and crushed by the weight of their mother's concern except they didn't get to smother to death they had to live with it. Anyway that day in Turkey was the best day of my life.

CENTERLINE

In the morning the centerline curves like the horizon—returns to itself as it circles my line of sight. Some lives have no centerline I've noticed. Maybe you've seen this too—even in yourself.

INUNDATION ZONE

In life you don't notice the inundation zone you've entered. A woman is walking down the street—crying—like an ordinary heartbroken person. Maybe her centerline is some loss she swerves across and back again—that loss that takes her head-on into everything moving against her—everything on its way to where she's already been.

Things that blow you sideways—pull you apart—wear you down—force you down—push you to the ground like shoves and hold you there—your face against the gravel—things like that don't come the way you think they will—from where you're looking I mean—they come from somewhere you're not thinking about at all. Like that pencil eraser you used and used when you were young and in school—a gradual coming apart until there was just the metal casing scratching the paper—those few final times you tried to use it anyway—the little grooves it made where you were trying to subtract your mistakes—and they could not be erased and trying only made things worse. That favorite pencil is what I'm talking about—the one with your teeth marks splitting the yellow paint—the one torn up like the golden road of your childhood.

CRACKS EVERYWHERE

The city's economy is mostly built on termites—fences falling down between houses—houses themselves like rows of rotting teeth. Cracks everywhere and widening—that person you almost started to like who had that little edge of finding fault and every time you saw her she found fault more and more—and everywhere people are stepping around those cracks the way at first you stepped around the find-fault in that person. You know the kind of day that's all jagged at the edges and the more you try to smooth it—file the edges down—the sharper they get? That time you were hammering something and you got enthusiastic because it was going so well and you hammered the nail right through into the table you were hammering on. That's pretty much the way being with that person you'd liked once was because when it was over you had to find a way to pry yourself apart from them and when you did the nail pretty much got ruined because you can't pull a nail straight out usually—it has to be bent to be removed—like comments you've made that you almost regret—how you have to bend them to retract them—but even after you do the hole is still there and the nail will never be straight again.

PAPER

Industrial coatings—cobalt—glycerin—silver—a metal mist refracts the sun at dawn. Your life folds into its form—is creased like paper formed to form a bird—or a fish—or something else that in life moves rapidly away.

PARALLEL OPPOSITES

On that highway of parallel opposites called *the self*—my buttons shine like coins from a parallel world—where emptiness is resolved through utility—resolved by a threading-through and a holding fast. Other emptiness is like that too you may have noticed—seeming to disappear when put to use.

I walk out into the morning. I trace the narrow edge of the familiar with my steps. Across some hidden boundary lies the great entirety of all that I will not reach. There is always that pull—back toward the familiar—there is an almost bodily yanking back—sometimes you shrug it off—like you shrug the grip of the cold from your shoulders with a shake before going forward.

TRACKS

They sell small segments of railroad track—the tracks that used to lead from the city—for paperweights at the river stalls. So now everyone can have a piece of getting out at a modest cost.

BUS TERMINAL

In the cardboard city—on a side street near the Square of Nothing—I found the old bus terminal. The fleet greyhound was drawn with a fine-point pencil and finished with smudged charcoal. The low-slung building filled about half a block—doors in rows stood at the back—long parking spaces for buses to load and leave.

NEEDLES

I am planning my trip to Needles. I imagine tall trees on both sides of the road before the land goes dusty and empty and flat. I imagine a certain kind of roadside store in those trees with jerky and tobacco tins and rubber flies for fishing and loaves of spongy white bread and richly scented plank floors and the person behind the counter a little gruff if a man and a little sweet if a woman but always tired in any case because keeping the place going well there's just so much to it isn't there.

TOURNIQUETS

I'm trying to figure out how to keep perspective and lend perspective at the same time. My friend says she has that bristlecone sore throat thing again. I wonder if a tourniquet might help.

BUS TERMINAL

I walk to the vacant lot where the terminal was. Now just some chairs grouped around coffee cans for cigarette butts. A few people milling around. Aimless chatter. I don't linger. Most things in the city—most people too—mean nothing to you—are like a clutch of things thrown through a wind tunnel. You try to find the things and people intended for you somehow—like some of the things you steal because they fit into a certain empty space that has opened at that moment in your life—an empty space shaped almost exactly like that thing—so much so you wonder sometimes if these objects or people or whatever actually opened that space the way your face opens a space just like itself on the surface of a mirror when you look there—or the way when you lower something into water it displaces it like the time your favorite doll was disloyal and you decided to drown her in the tub drown her in cold water the coldest water you could run with not a drop of warm not a drop—the eyes looking up at you from underneath—expressionless—well maybe just a muffled hint of stark surprise a kind of hint of *how could you* but maybe not—those eyes from underneath—that look—you've since seen that look so often on bus after bus—that muffled slightly incredulous expressionless look from underneath the cold bath of lives and how did these people get under there and whose hand was holding each under and was it the hand of someone they'd once thought loved them.

THE GLASS-EYED BLIND

The city is a story that's handed to you—whole and in motion—a story you find your way in—or lose your way in—or sit on stone steps and watch.

You've noticed them I know—glass-like eyes that see no one—eyes locked like little deadbolts—everywhere more and more. A way to notice nothing—as if the eyes were glass—a glass-eyed blindness—something like that—as if the eyes were Squares of Nothing that everyone sees through—or a game of being spun around blindfolded—*where is the world*—and the light from those glassy eyes—too sharp—like the uncaring edge of a paring knife in the hands of a child cutting onions distractedly.

On the streetcar the glass-eyed blind sit and stand—jostle and hold on—keep distances—keep quiet—look by looking away—a lockstep kind of seeing like strides coincide when people walk side-by-side. The glass-eyed blind are still persons mostly I think—the way the mirror of the dead is still mostly a mirror.

UNDERWORLD

I tried it on that this was the underworld. The thought clung like fire to the skin of a saint.

I learned to make my eyes look glass-eyed-blind—so as not to stand out—so as not to be noticed as one who noticed things.

In hell the clocks run backwards—so the longer you are there the longer you have to be there. Like the kingdom of red ribbons—where the more you cut away of yourself the more yourself you seem—this is a lying-mirror kind of place.

Some sections of the city have been given over entirely to the dust. You would think the implosions would shake the houses but they don't. You would think that concrete floors descending into rubble would make a thunderous noise but it's not so. All is muted here—in this city of muffled drumming—a drumming like distant fingers on a desktop in a room where a decision is pending and pending.

INSIDE OUT

Dr. Winker says I have an *inside out* or an *outside in* sort of problem. He can't make up his mind which one it is. The building collapsing on the corner is collapsing in here—*in me.* The building being demolished down the street is being demolished in me. In my heart the furious salt-laden waves are pouring their weight downward in great arcs. The leaves in gales are flying between the trees and the trees and the spaces between them and the leaves and the gales are in here. You know—like that time you were struck by lightning and the outside and the inside were the same at least in that instant and in that instant that boundary being gone illuminated you somehow—well—illuminated wasn't exactly it but you get the idea. Anyway Dr. Winker says people know where they start and stop but I don't. As usual he's wrong. I start where I'm standing and I stop at the horizon—just like everybody else.

TWISTS AND TURNS

So many nameless streets. So many twists and turns—steps folded back on themselves—like footings slipping on shale. People like robbed shelves—emptied shelves—houses abandoned to winters and winters and winters.

SAINTS

Every saint makes something new of the truth—that's the point. I made the angel-child the *Saint of the Square of Nothing*. I made Aspergum the *Saint of the Chains we Choose*. I made overhead bus wires the *Saints of the Lost Songs of Birds*.

MIRROR WORKS

The Mercury Mirror Works on Midwick Street stands mostly empty. Maybe people just don't want to look at themselves anymore.

WALL OF THE LOST

Now only the changing light inhabits the Wall of the Lost and the changing light leaves no message or maybe just the message about how light comes and goes—the way the seconds come and go—but the seconds do not come back to The Wall of the Lost.

ANGEL CHILD

I meant to tell you. A child was standing in the Square of Nothing—a girl—in an angel costume—tattered yellowed wings branched out behind her—*something from a trunk in an attic* I thought—*when there were such things*—and in her hands held out and being shook was a sheet of foil. A kind of splintery multicolored music fired forth—the notes—like breaking glass—shot across that empty space. I stood very still—looked around—waited and watched. The city was just the same and the faces the same and the things people did were the same—as if going through a windshield had severed the nerves of your face so your face was frozen in a single flat expression—so the city remained expressionless—blank and settled—like scars.

Whatever falls into your hands brings its weight with it—its need to be carried. Any gift—any wealth—any calling—any beauty—any awakening—whatever it is it comes with its burdensome bulk. You don't think of this when you wish—crave—envy—seek. You think getting what you want will exact no price. This is the promise of desire that attainment never keeps.

In the shattered-glass music I saw that something could be different. I went into the streets—that song behind me—pressing me forward. I'm sure you've had thoughts like these—about changing everything.

FAIRY TALE

In the fairy tale the girl found another continuity in herself like that time you went down into your basement and found a cold stream flowing there and couldn't remember if it had always been there or had you put your bare feet in it before and where did it come from where was the source and you got down on your knees and you pressed your lips to those waters and it lifted you into yourself and out of yourself like the miracle of the first mirror and you were not the same again and you knew it right away and then you never wanted to drink from anywhere else and then you noticed that stream wasn't just in your basement it was everywhere—that you were fording it endlessly—that you were putting your lips to it over and over again.

BOUNDARIES

I tried to remember to notice what was missing. I noticed that certain clouds were now extinct—couldn't form in the torpor above this place—the icy wispy distant ones that used to mark the boundaries of the sky.

Slowly I started to tell myself the truth—to stay away from all the stories that lead down dead sidings—to find that narrow truthful track somewhere in the switchyard of lies that had become my life.

FREEZER

I noticed a kind of tidal lock—how people turned from themselves —became people they weren't—lost sight of their lost other sides—lived lives not even at arm's length—how the underworld stood in for those lives that were over—unfolded seamless as shame—same as salt—airtight like that unplugged freezer I dreamed I could use to teach my cousin to play hide and seek in a way she'd never be found.

COMETS

Maybe you don't know much about comets. I didn't either. You may think a comet comes and goes and that is that. This is not so. A comet leaves a dust trail that the earth passes through on its orbit twice a year—a trail of particles—most no larger than sand—struck where they stand in earth's path—flashing across the sky as shooting stars.

THE PAST IS PATIENT

I've never seen the sea be phosphorescent but I read about it once. My father thought the world was mostly cardboard. *Only what glitters matters* he would say. Sometimes everything glittered—even cardboard.

The past is patient. It waits up ahead for you to arrive. It waits where your life will carry you into collisions of ice and fire—cold memories—struck and ignited.

There in a pawnshop window—the antique copper compass my father traded for a Gila monster—*they're illegal to own you know*—and the Gila monster was docile except when you put it on the marble coffee table and its temperature dropped and it started spinning and hissing like something was coming at it from all sides—you know the way madness does—comes at you from all sides I mean—writhing and whipping its head and tail around and trying to bite your fingers off *you know they won't let go* he said *even if you cut off their head—you might as well just cut your fingers off.*

WALL OF THE LOST

Everyone has a *Wall of the Lost* inside themselves somewhere—pictures—pathways—events that start and stop like movies at the Pix. Everyone passes that wall every day because it's not in a single place. It stands opposite your life—always. You know how in dreams you never question things no matter how strange things get—having parents is like that in a way—when you're small.

We were deposed royalty being pursued by assassins. We were food critics. We were friends of the famous. We were a rotary of endless random doublings.

The mirror of the dead remembers everything in reverse—that time you cut your own hair and cut it and cut it and it was still too short. Maybe your memories advance in your thoughts through turnstiles—one at a time. Maybe your memories don't force doors—aren't rocks thrown through windows—aren't shoulders slamming doors you've closed and locked—slamming and splintering everything as they break and enter—burglars in reverse—not breaking in to take the things you'll miss—but breaking in to leave them.

WORLDS RISING AND FALLING

We were on a train. The compartment was empty except for us. My father was reading a newspaper. I was looking out the window. Everything unwound—one of those intermission moments. The train rocked back and forth—a slow-motion metronome—marking hours in miles—worlds rising and falling away—landscapes—towns—the backs of houses with laundry hung on lines—kids playing in yards—everything momentary—almost instantly gone.

You find yourself in moments like that—carried in stillness against the deluge. The ever more distant origins somehow recede and remain—remain and change—like light. You find yourself in that forward and backward way—the fulcrum of all that lasts and all that can't.

MIRROR-WORKS

I hid that backpack I told you about—the one I'll escape with—the one stuffed with sweaters and food like meals for astronauts—behind a stack of empty frames at the mirror-works.

FAIRY TALE

A fairy tale is not just a story of finding your way back—it's a means of finding your way back. Distance is the difference—up close you can only work in inches—work to pull yourself out like that figure you saw trying to struggle free from that block of marble that time.

In the fairy tale the girl did not surrender the buttons to the gods on Scissor Days. She hid them in the desk drawers of abandoned buildings—in cupboards of deserted houses—under garbage cans in parks—in the coatroom cubbies of deserted schools. She hoarded them by hiding them—doubled as indifferent to them—doubled as someone throwing them away. She walled the buttons off the way you wall off parts of yourself you think are beautiful because the clumsy world will sully them. She hid the buttons coldly—the way sometimes you can see yourself in cold light—you are not kidding yourself at all—you are hiding nothing from yourself—you know what this is going to mean—how this will end—you go forward anyway—you go forward like glaciers—knowing you tear up the ground you walk across.

VOICE

Dr. Winker says I've become *selectively mute*. He doesn't know that speaking is a threshold. He doesn't know all that is lost—that dissipates—when you cross that line—how all those held-in things—that make your walls—escape when you speak. He doesn't see that a world unsaid is a world that has not been split apart and broken apart and spilled on the floor everywhere.

NUN

I tried on being a nun for a night—walked through a doorway where doubt is what you forget—entered the claustrophobia of faith—there on my narrow hard bed. I settled into that tight plain purifying life—let the weight of it descend—there on the hard narrow bed of that belief—that faith—held in place by some greater obligation that confers liberation by removing choice. On my nun-bed I wondered—*what if the rapture doesn't happen for a really long long time and there isn't much of me left—maybe just a molecule or two*—and there against the hard starless dark of that closed-casket ceiling I thought *maybe the lord doesn't need that much to work with.*

BOOKMARKS

I found a book with photos inserted as bookmarks—ordinary pictures of people—people standing shoulder to shoulder—some smiling—some not—some smiles forced as is always the case with such things. I sat on the floor of my room and studied them. On the inside cover was the message—*please return to such and such a person at such and such address*—and I thought I knew where that was even though many house numbers are no longer where they were—and I wrapped the book in brown paper with cobalt glitter I'd gathered by hand from the streets and tightly tied it with expensive twine I'd stolen and put a note inside and cancelled stamps on the front and walked with it through the streets in the dark so as not to be seen and left it on that doorstep—leaned it up against the door actually—and I never heard a thing from them—not a word of thanks—nothing.

VOICE

Dr. Winker says I've misplaced my voice. He doesn't know that speaking is like uncorking a beaker of ether—how everything inside evaporates and every outside thing is suctioned into sleep.

FAIRY TALE

When abandoned buildings were slated for demolition the girl would go in and search for the buttons she'd hidden from the gods—and retrieve them—those that she could find—and carry them out—in her pockets—in cookie tins—in small cloth bags—in her clenched fists—and hide them in other buildings. She'd mark where the buttons were hidden on the quilted secret map under which she slept—sometimes with pinned foil she'd found—or with glued clumps of glitter gathered from beside the railroad tracks—or she'd sew a collar button right on the spot. When buildings were about to come down—even after the dynamite was set—she'd be in there looking and looking—the way people in their last hours look hard across their histories for something to redeem them—redeem their lives I mean. Sometimes she failed—barely getting out—and the buildings came down with the buttons in them—the way lives come down sometimes with dreams of other lives hidden somewhere inside. Sometimes she sifted the rubble for buttons—sometimes she found a few—usually none. The gods found her out. Memories chopped like snatched cars—partials taken for wholes—splintered lath and plaster taken for walls.

BOOK CLUB

The book club president let me know—after I'd gone twice—that they had several *exit packages* from which to choose. It must've been something I didn't say. I think the twitchy lady with the bad eyeliner did me in—always on the edge of a complaint and always my problem to solve or I was the problem that no one could solve but me and what was I going to do about it *right away* is what was meant what was I going to do about the problem I'd become and what was I going to do about it *now?*

She should pray that I am not the one who kills her. If I kill her it will be in error—in misses—in slips. She should pray a perfect prayer with no syllable out of place that a bungler like myself will not kill her. I will listen at the door—I will listen with rapt attention to the tenor of her voice to the treaty her tongue would make with what gods there are—to the pleading pushed far back behind a front of tenderness. She is not going to escape with a prayer like that. I will be at the door when she finishes. I will be at the door—patient as a pocketknife. I will hear the Amen if there is one.

Anyway the club president said that on my departure I could get a canvas tote with the book club's motto *read, read, and read*—which sounded to me like a law firm—or a pocket dictionary—or a lanyard. I didn't know what a lanyard was but it sounded nautical so I went with that. As I left—the club members assured me that they did not want me to stop reading.

ROCK

I went to the sand mine and stood in the haywire wind. How far can you throw a rock—you can't help but throw one as hard as you can. In the great blank space across the mine pit you can't even tell how far it carries before it falls. Listen as intently as you can—you will not know when it lands—there are none who will ever know.

ROWING

The lanyard turned out to be a nylon cord for a nametag. I should have taken the tote. I guess I don't have *both oars in the water* as they say. This matters when you row alone.

TORN THREADS

When it comes to being alive—whatever idea you have—it's not enough. You don't know how much of everything is nothing when you run your life like a ribbon through your fingers—you don't know how discontinuous things are.

The gods tore the threads that tied my thoughts to things and things to events and events to my life in that way that things you've done belong to you and are not the stories you've heard or the things that happened to someone else or the things that you've made up. So were my memories torn from me—like that child you lost in that riptide that time in bright sun when the sand burned your feet as you carried her to the sea—and all the life-charge left behind in buttons—fastened thoughtlessly by fingers urgent with tasks—now turned against me like when you claw your cheeks to ribbons in your sleep. I had hidden the buttons coldly. You cannot betray the gods without consequence. What are you willing to forget to remember beauty?

FANCIFUL THINGS

I used to think some very fanciful things. The world will wring that out of you you know. The world will give you things to replace those fanciful things like a pack rat in your mountain cabin will leave you things not as good for the various things it's taken.

WHAT MUST HAPPEN

Fate always arrays itself on the side of what must happen. Lies stack up between you and someone else—lots of lies—and the house you've made is that house of crackers you built when you were a child with the cracker ramp leading up to the parking platform on the cracker roof and when you rolled that big red metal truck up that ramp and parked that truck on that roof the house collapsed.

ROWING

I know my father rows a small glass boat beneath the surf. Deep in the sea I know he rows and rows—bent to that task in the turbulent dark. I know there is no boat beneath the sea that my father rows. I know there is no land that he could reach—pulling oars—stiff as the open empty hands of the dead—against the tides.

Do you ever wonder how many miles to shore—bent to your life—oars in hand—pulling and reaching and pulling—how many miles? Do you say the shore is tomorrow—next week—next year—do you look for that shore in every conversation—every glance—every Monday Friday circuit that you make—every hour you lie awake rowing and rowing from one day toward the next?

When someone you have loved walks into the sea—any sea—sea of voices—sea of strangers—sea of sounds—how many miles of shoreline will you walk as you search for them? You can make a life of what you find along the way—things thrown to shore—things hurled landward—things discarded—spat up by the surf—thrown down by hands—shells broken or whole.

The boat of the dead is glass because death is completely see-through. The dead are transparent too if you think about it. The longer they are dead the more transparent they become until they are perfectly clear—clear like the coldest morning when you rise and your feet hit the cold floor and you know you are alive. In that moment of being solid—you stand next to all the see-through things—vivid against the cold. The dead are clear as that morning—a clarity immediate as that. When you stand in that cold by the bed where you slept you will know how being alive stands by being dead—how sharply the two abut.

FAIRY TALE

The girl knew that she couldn't hide and keep the buttons any longer—that her memory would be emptied of everything. She had to stop—the way when the last few things you have are sliding from that table you've been tilting and you stop. She determined that she must get rid of the buttons—throw them from a bridge—let the current take them away.

DRAWINGS OF EVERYTHING MISSING

I stole a sketchpad and a box of colored pencils and some pastels from that abandoned art supply store I think it was. I drew the wind buffeting all the birds that were missing. I drew gravestones—lots of gravestones—on low-rolling hills—all the kinds of gravestones I could think of—even those of the very rich in their grandeur—even those of children—young children—even the barely born—even the simplest gravestones with scarcely room for a name and a pair of dates—even stones with the names worn off by the weather. I drew them and drew them. I drew music shaken from foil across the Square of Nothing—the notes like razors—sharp and shiny. Children—I drew children—running and playing and I made voice-balloons around them full of all the shrieks and screams of joy they could not contain and they were tumbling down grass hillsides and climbing trees and riding bikes and playing horse and playing bird and the sun was high so you could see that it was summer and you couldn't help but remember the seasons then and how they came and went and how the children loved them each and all. People talking to each other and touching each other I drew these people these people embracing whom I had never seen but noticed that they were missing and remembered what it had been like to see people embrace in the world before this world.

I called these drawings *my drawings of everything missing* and I taped them to the Wall of the Lost to remind everyone who passed of what was missing. All these drawings—all these drawings of all the things I'd noticed that were missing—I'm telling you I tore them from my sketchpad and I taped them to the Wall of the Lost for all the glass-eyed-blind to see—to remind them—to make them remember—to get them to notice that they were in the underworld. I drew a flock of birds and then another and another and I taped these drawings to the Wall of the Lost and I drew the clouds that were now extinct and I placed them above the rest.

MAP

The last time I saw my father. All I can remember is the cold. Cold as the light the snow casts into your room when you wake in the newly made winter. Cold as fate is what I'm talking about.

One day the Gila monster shed its beautiful beaded skin—pink and black—and I folded it in fourths—placed it in one of the secret pockets I'd sewn inside my coat—and it was like having a small topographical map—or a message in braille—from a faraway other place—of how to get there—if I could just figure out how to read it.

THE FATES

I went to the Pix on the last night of its life. The movie being shown—about the Fates—was a silent film—jerky and grainy—with those exaggerated movements actors make when more accustomed to stage than screen. The subtitles were large and white in a kind of dated cursive like the cursive on that chart that hung on the wall of my classroom when I was a child and my classmates were all shuffling and restless in their seats and the chalk squeaked on the blackboard—the blackboard that at the end of the day would be written on by someone who'd misbehaved—or fallen asleep—some words again and again—a kind of prayer or promise or other incantation to the little gods that manage little classrooms—and then the following morning the board would be clean and flat and blank as a beach when the tide has gone out and you are the first to set foot on it just after dawn. A cursive like that was under the fleeting choppy images on the screen at the Pix that night and the Three Fates were spinning the thread of life and apportioning it and cutting it with huge scissors and the mortal in the film was at first a girl and then a woman and then was old and at the end was terrified and trying to get away but she ended up dead on her bed with a Lilac on her chest and gray coins on her eyes. Maybe myth is a way to talk about what's true in a way that gives it meaning—like identity is a way to talk about your self that's more meaningful than true.

THE PIX

They demolished the Pix this morning. It didn't take much. In the cardboard city I cut the theatre from the plywood and disassembled it piece by piece—the walls—the wire—the foil—the glittery marquee. I thought I'd make a boat of these disparate parts—the small boat you bail with bare hands—and place it in the current of *The River of No Going Back*—but you can't fashion a boat out of just about anything—so tonight I'll take the parts to the ruined lot—burn what will burn—bury the rest.

BLISTERING WIND

You can't finally put the world back the way it was. Even in miniature. A blistering wind scoured the streets to a polished white like flies clean carcass bones—swept the cardboard buildings from their sites—stripped everything I'd placed on the Wall of the Lost—the clouds—the children—the birds—the notes of music—the gravestones—everything torn away. You look for the scattered remnants. Don't even bother.

NEEDLES

I went to the car lot on Trampas Street at the end of the streetcar line across from what used to be *For Christ's Sake* Catholic Church now long abandoned. A salesman sidled up to me and I gave him my contest-winner-authorization-letter to test-drive a car of my choice to Needles and back. He barely gave it a glance before crushing it into the pocket of his freshly lacquered sports coat—*Needles?*—he ventured vaguely—and then he started that fork-fingered up and down *I can make you a deal* kind of hand motion as he rolled his lingo across me like a grass-killing plastic tarp. Anyway—*No credit—No Problem* turned out not to be the same as *No credit—No cash—No license—No Problem*—so after some back and forth during which he assured me he was doing everything he could to *get me into a car* it all came to nothing and I walked.

FAITH

I crossed the street and went into the old church looking for something left on the floor—or in a nook—or behind a pew—maybe a hymnal or some of that special flare-red glass they used to use to cup the memory candles—the ones people lit for the dead or to make a special request—the ones in tiered rows with the small wooden donation box beside them.

You know the way churches are not like other abandoned places and not quite like theatres and not like auditoriums at all and not like abandoned train stations—things down to the bare walls you'd think would be alike but they aren't. Lives down to the bare walls are more alike than these I think. That house of crackers I was telling you about—that couldn't take the weight—I think when faith falls it falls like that.

FATE

You don't know what the wind is really doing until it picks something up in front of you. As I left the church I saw a gray plastic bag lift off—twist—invert—almost pirouette—and come to rest again on the pavement at my feet. You don't know what the wind is doing until it picks something up. Fate is like that too.

IV

The Second Language of Leaving

COMPANY PARTY

The past is patient. Stone eagles stood on either side of stone steps leading up to a building no longer standing. I stood between them. I knew this place. We went to the company party here—when the still-somewhat-utilized lodge had just started its tilt toward decline. The room had seemed vast. Everything tawdry but trying to be everyday-decent—glittery streamers—random flag bunting—foil chocolates left over from Christmas. The smell of mold had only the slightest toehold in the room—soon to be washed aside in perfume and loud men's cologne. Posters of the company's products were taped to the walls—*custom cold-formed fasteners—rivet setting machines.* My mother went grudgingly but did her best—once there—to be genial. There was a bar—tickets handed out for the first two drinks—cash after that—proceeds to some cheerless children's charity I think it was. There was a dance floor with tables around it. A man in a turquoise sports coat played dated records through big speakers. The aluminum steam-tray buffet offered spaghetti in red sauce—Caesar salad—soppy garlic bread—and some sort of plastic pudding for dessert. Beneath the shopworn glitz there was a goodness—round and full—of people who belonged to each other. My father was peddling hard to keep up with what all the others already had—a place in that world. He darted from person to person—making small talk—asking leading questions about kids and schools and kids' sports—everything buzzing and positive like florescent lights. I could see the cost on his face—the rainbow sheen on the surface—the black pool beneath. The awards came during dinner—after the raffled weekend at the owner's lakeside cabin. They weren't *awards* exactly—just proclamations—certificates and applause. *Salesman of the year—Most new accounts*—you get the idea. People sat with people they'd sat with for years. The newer employees bunched in distant orbits from the center. When names were announced—the men—it was always men—popped from their seats with feigned—who me?—surprised-looks on their faces. My father stared into space. When he was named *Most-Improved Salesman* he slightly gasped and smiled and waved to everyone as he went to the front of the room to receive his award and shake the owner's hand. He sat back down with a thud—his right arm stretched across the table like someone giving blood. Early in the evening—just as the dancing started—we left.

GLISTENING RAILS

Have you ever noticed how it's just in the nature of things to get tangled—threads—thoughts—conversations—extension cords—explanations—excuses—stories—lies—lives—and you can't even start—anything—without the work of untangling what's already there—I mean the things you need to get started are tangled to start with and you can only start right away if you don't mind tangling things more. I often started that way—tangling things more—my father taught me how—and when things were just too tangled to continue there were always trains—how train tracks always untangle everything—those glistening directional rails headed straight to somewhere—always leaving everything tangled behind. Some people are born wanting to get away. Even as a child I wanted to escape my past—even though I mostly hadn't even had it yet.

PILGRIMS

Memories are like teeth—they don't get better on their own. We stood in the station at Maastricht—my father wanted to find a very old church with a basement and a sub-basement and be medieval pilgrims coming from far away—carrying almost nothing—seeking religious relics—saint's bones and pieces of the cross—things like that to pray to and maybe convince the presiding priest to let us touch them and maybe even clutch them to our hearts. *You'll have some wasting disease—something in the blood that cannot be cured—You will be ecstatic* he said—*You will be touched by Christ.* The church we find is a thousand years old. I think the priest is younger. I am not ecstatic. I am not touched by Christ. The priest is not convinced.

FAIRY TALES

I'm sure you know the fairy tale about the man who always wanted more—the man who demanded that another line be crossed on his behalf—again and again and again and none ever enough—how the yielding and yielding hardened into a fierce digging-in—like someone being dragged across rough ice—and then a kind of giving up like just before you drown—when drowning has you fully in its grip. Or maybe you know the fairy tale of the girl who had to find a way to stay alive by telling stories in the house in the woods with the demon and the knives and the always winter outside.

I don't want to have to remind you of why this matters. How I just wanted to keep to the right side of the cyclone—things torn up—shredded—thrown everywhere—just over there—on the other side of that line—that mentally chalked perimeter—to be just out of view when the mayhem started up—the reflexive impulse to point away from yourself—toward anywhere toward anyone—just so long as you were not the noticed—the brought forward—the sighted—the one fixed in the crosshairs of that storm where something always needed breaking before the storm itself would break.

LOSS

Loss isn't all at once every time—sometimes it arrives like bleeding when you've cut yourself through your clothes.

COMPANY PARTY

After the company party—driving home—there was mostly silence. The sullen aftermath of acquiescing to *people of no account* as my father called them—*crossword puzzle people—fill-in-the-boxes for a life and erase until you get it right* kind of people—and we were not that kind of people—and we had to pander just to survive in this *crossword-puzzle-world.* My mother glanced from the road—*you don't have to be disdainful*—she said wearily—*they're just trying to make a living and get along.* This only made things worse. *As if life were just about getting along* my father said—his volume rising—she sighed and looked away. The certificate—torn to shreds—went out the passenger window.

OVER

What do you do when your life is over—I mean the way you've been living it—the same chair—the same window—the same food over and over—the same conversations just rearranged to slightly freshen them—you have to find a way through the habit and humdrum—somewhere between the clicks of the metronome—a doorway—to forget the dead life you are trying to leave—you don't keep knitting that life in that automatic way that people knit when they sit with others and need something to do with their hands—you put all that down and you get up and you walk.

LIONS

One night I slept where they'd kept the lions at the now abandoned zoo—terraces of gray rock—some boulders to hide behind—the fences ragged as picked prey—the mote empty and cracked—grasses protruding through fissures in the pavement. I had no lion dreams. I had no special sense that they had been there. In the morning I was sore and stiff and cold and the same. Sometimes you tell yourself something should matter but you can't make it matter no matter what.

TRACKS

I thought some railroad tracks might lead out of town. I tried to follow them but rail-tie monotony stopped me—or something distracted me—some district shimmering with spent purposes and opportunities to rifle.

I'm not going to be hard to understand if I can help it. No harder than nighttime or moonlight or gravity or brittle or blue-green. The thing is so much seems to happen all at once—so much sorting of things with no labels—things with no right-side up.

MOTEL RADIO

My friend is like one of those motel radio alarm clocks that was set and left by whoever had the room before you had it and now it's going off in the middle of the night and you don't know what it is at first and you're struggling to find a way to turn it off and the song is loud and always something about a man who did his woman dirty wrong and wants her to take him back I would never take him back I would beat him to pulp with the handle of the payphone he's calling from I would beat him down in that phone booth I would break the glass with the back of his head I would break his ankles to bits in the collapsing metal door I would steal his car and wreck it and pull myself out of that wreckage and walk away and I would never take him back.

I walk the side streets littered and shining. I wander through overgrown gardens. I go to the ocean some evenings—one step—one step—one step along the shore. The somersaulting waters of the waves remind me how foreign a thing it is to be alive—how strange it is.

GOLD ANCHOR PIN

The past is patient—like matches it waits to be struck—on an ordinary day—on a side street—in a shop—in a garden—on a beach you walk that curves away out of sight.

I saw a woman wearing my mother's gold anchor pin—the one my father gave her when they were still speaking sort of—the one that provided the single-word instruction for who she was to be for him. My mother must have torn the pin off and thrown it down when she left—maybe in the street outside the house—maybe in the cab she took—maybe in a park where she sat on a bench and watched the weather churn and break and move and knew that it was over.

Things are broken up like that sometimes—broken to bits—like streets divided by bigger streets and former schools and parks that divide them from themselves like certain tropical worms that severed into parts lead separate lives. You can't count all the doors on all those broken streets—when things are over— you can't notice door after door—each featureless as numbness before it wakes—each lost like something the same is lost in all things like it.

I did not follow the woman wearing the anchor pin. I did not care who she was or where she got it. I returned to the lodge-site and sat on the hard stone steps. It was not like trying to sleep where the lions had slept. It was not about trying to sleep in any way. It was not that hard emptiness of trying to make things matter that can't matter.

The way light bends and splinters and persists as it rises from depths is the way my memories came to me that day—how the phone began ringing incessantly—ringing and ringing. You see my mother was an answer-the-phone kind of person and my father was not—it hadn't mattered because the black rotary phone on the phone table in the hall rarely rang—until it did—and did—and did—and my mother would answer and have words with someone and hang up abruptly and then it would ring again and this went on and on and one evening as the phone was ringing my mother turned to my father and said—*You have to handle this*—and my father did not *handle this*—and mid-ring my mother went over to the phone and picked it up and tore it from the wall and slammed it to the floor and stormed from the house.

FIRE-CLOCKS

We were on a train. The tidy-type man sitting across from us in the compartment grew nervous and quizzical the way discomfort sometimes forces you to speak. He said he sold candy—wholesale—offered me a piece of cheap public chocolate—and asked my father what he did for a living. *I make fire-clocks* my father said. *You can make a fire-clock of anything if you know its combustion rate and have a means to light it* he said in his *if you're bright you'll agree with me* voice. *If I knew exactly what your house was made of I could make a fire-clock of your house.* The man was not amused— *but usually we're talking about candles and incense sticks* my father continued undeterred. *But you might want to know if you have a six-hour house or a ten-hour house or a twenty-four-hour house because your watches may burn if your house burns and how will you know the time? I'm not including accelerants in this discussion of course—or friction-fires where mortgages rub against insurance policies.* The man began to squirm—*your body is a fire-clock burning steadily* my father said—*if you knew what you were made of you'd know how long you'd live—oh—I also sell fire insurance.* Excuse me—the candy wholesaler said hurriedly—and departed the compartment. My father stretched out and put his feet on the seat across from him where the man had been.

DARK-PLACE BLUE

The sky was dark-place blue. That thing in the dark when the train windows turn into mirrors so your compartment is next to you—riding along outside. You're next to yourself as well—out there in the dark. I became afraid that we would never find home—our life of arriving nowhere. My father said—*I want to talk to you about that—after we say goodbye.*

Why do you think things that are farther away look smaller when they aren't? Do you really understand why this happens—I don't. Some things in the past grow bigger and bigger the farther away they get. My father's fire-clock life. I stared at my reflection in the window of that train—everything happening behind me in slow motion. Turnstiles of selves—turnstiles of souls brought into our doubling-circles—horizon after horizon.

STARRY BRIGHT

I found the Starry Bright Motel on a street in the cardboard city—a side street actually—in a rundown district where mostly I think traveling salesmen and their paid companions landed like ships—wrecked against rocks—in the splintered unnavigable nights that marked the shorelines of their lives. The motel was built meticulously—precisely cut cardstock—a tarpaper parking lot—the second-floor gallery in front of the row of rooms—each numbered—the railing a fashioned lattice of bent wires. Cigarette-foil letters—cut with scissors tiny as those you'd find in a dollhouse sewing room—adorned a cardboard marquee. Vacancy was stamped in red below.

I knew the walk would take hours. I didn't know if the motel was even still standing. This didn't stop me. I drew a map with a few scattered landmarks noted. I took my flashlight and a packet of extra batteries just in case. I took my folding straight razor. I took Aspergum. I took water.

I arrived near dark as planned. The motel looked like it should have been condemned. Some rooms had lights on. Most did not. There were people living there—squatters I thought—some raucous and wailing—some laughing—screaming—throwing things. I knew there were others—seated on floors—pressed into corners—silent—knees tucked up—staying away from the windows —waiting for the tumult to pass. I wanted to go unnoticed—impossibly unimportant—invisible. I walked up the concrete stairs to the second-floor gallery with its rickety railing—lengths of it now missing—and walked down the row of rooms—yes—this was the one.

ROULETTE

Memory has a thousand doors—a thousand rooms—but each is one at a time—like one card at a time in solitaire—or one bullet at a time from a revolver—that man I hardly knew—that man who was the helper of the repairman living next to us—who I saw several times in the passenger seat of that truck and was introduced to me maybe once or twice but in memory his face is formless and then one day I heard that he had died though he was young and strong and I was told the circumstances were uncertain or—to be more exact—barely spoken of—but it was rumored he'd died playing Russian roulette. Russian roulette. And I wondered suddenly what had been underneath—underneath that soft clipped speech—not much to say it seemed—and was it just a drunken dare—a crazy impulse—or was it the way out he'd been looking for—the exit ramp from the must do and the must have and possessions gathered and stacked like bodies in a plague.

THE ARC OF DISENCHANTMENT

The door to the room where my mother and I had stayed was standing open. I entered and tried the lights but nothing happened. I pulled the yellowed curtains back and in the last light saw how almost nothing can nonetheless be completely disarrayed.

Legs of a bedside table lay on the floor like cudgels. A mattress sagged against a far wall where it had been thrown. Another mattress—frameless—sideways as a fitful sleep—lay slung on the floor. This had been my mother's mattress that night. I pulled the other down from against the wall—dragged it over and dropped it roughly where it had been—across from hers. No sheets pillows or blankets needless to say. I lay down and looked at the ceiling.

My life of looking had started here—on this mattress—my life of looking and looking and being lost and not giving up no matter what. My mother had driven me to the Starry Bright Motel with little notice—no notice actually. She came into my room like someone repossessing things bought on credit—pulling a pink duffle bag from my closet—emptying its contents on the floor—telling me to pack essentials and hurry. I packed some pants—some underwear—a shirt or two—no time to waste—my toothbrush—a comb—you get the idea. Minutes later we were in the car cruising quickly through the city as the sun was setting.

Have you ever been being taken somewhere and you don't know where and you don't know why and you're looking out the car window and you are seeing things go by but you're not seeing where you are—this turn—that turn—fast and emphatic and all you are actually seeing are the questions blanketing everything—and you're heading into some part of the city where you've never been before and it's all happening outside your life somehow in a way that makes everything hard to locate and keep—the way you can't keep things when you're hurtling through them.

We drove and drove and I hadn't even known the city went on this far. Drug stores with people loitering outside—smoking and talking—fast food places with people huddled together at small tables or waiting in cars in line at the pick-up window—bars—lots of bars with no windows—some with doors that looked like they'd been through sieges—some with doors padded like cells for the insane—bouncers in front of some of them—women smoking cigarettes—looking listless and bored in front of others. Fewer and fewer houses. More and more apartments—mostly run-down—small loose laughing groups of people standing around on corners—leaning on cars—couples wearing leather jackets walking quickly and leaning into each other as night fell fast.

All this activity eventually thinned and we entered some industrial desert with closed warehouses and wrecking yards and wholesale distributors with bays for trucks and guard-dogs patrolling the fenced loading areas. All the while we were turning—right left right—the way you drive when you're looking for something and you're not sure where it is. The *Vacancy* sign was lit at the Starry Bright Motel and we turned abruptly into the parking lot. My mother did not leave me in the car when she got the room in the cramped little office with the coffee pot and the cigarette machine and the manager sizing us up. Behind the desk—through a doorway—you could see into the living quarters where a TV was playing a rerun of some game show and people were bunched on a couch drinking sodas and eating chips.

Our room was on the second floor—facing the parking lot. We went up the concrete stairs with the metal railing and we stood on the gallery while my mother tried to get the key to work and eventually she did and we went in. You didn't want to be in that room with its two twin beds and no art on the walls and the lamp that didn't work. We sat opposite each other on the beds—our feet nearly touching in the narrow space between them. She said we needed to get a few things straight and then she flew into her speech like someone pushed from behind off a cliff. She said that the company started calling—looking for my father—calling and calling—and he wouldn't answer the phone and he wouldn't come to the phone and he wouldn't call them back so they talked to her. All those contracts he'd supposedly closed had started coming back. Broken—all broken. False promises—phony pricing—

impossible guarantees—one customer didn't even exist I think she said and she was rambling about lies all lies and how did he think it would ever work itself out and then she said that a woman started calling—that woman he'd married before he'd married her and she was sorry to have to tell me but that woman was my mother—my actual mother—and now she and my father were not even married because that woman wasn't dead and they'd never divorced so now she and my father were not even nothing and she said that woman was coming for what was hers after years of trying to find us.

Stunned as hammers I stared at the stains in the carpet—how like continents they were—the seas between them. I nodded. Said nothing. She rose and went to the window—her back to me—staring out into the parking lot. She said how he couldn't support me for long anyway—down to the last of the old money and nothing he *really did*. We wouldn't be in that rental house for long—he wouldn't face things—he'd run—dragging me with him—just as he always had—the way he'd run from that woman—dragging me along.

She paused like someone pauses after stumbling—*Coming to get what's hers*—she repeated pointlessly—*I have to leave*. She turned—came back—sat back down on the bed and I think she said something—ruefully—about magicians and escape artists—the one becoming the other—but I may have made that up because I couldn't keep hearing her because I'd fallen into that muffled sea between the stains. I know she said that this was where it ends—that *arc of disenchantment* I think it was—ends here on this hard thin mattress—here in this room or one just like it—staring at these bare walls. She told me to take a look around—to take it all in—because this was where it ends. She wouldn't look at me. She stared at the ceiling—her hands in her lap. I rose like some string-pulled thing and bent to hug her and then I sat back down on my bed. She said that in the morning she was getting in that car and driving off and not coming back and she was willing to take me with her even though I wasn't really hers and we'd make a new life somewhere away from all these lies away from this life of lies that was my father's life and she told me to get some rest because we'd be leaving early.

I lay awake a long time. I mean I never slept. Sometime in the night I got up—having never removed my clothes—except for my shoes which I grabbed—and I left my used-to-be-my-mother asleep in that motel room. The streets were dark and endless and unfamiliar. I made my way—I don't remember how—back to my father's house.

UNDER THE ICE

Lying in that motel room again—in that space disjoined by time from the past it held—on that mattress again—in the demolition-derby-mayhem of colliding lives. I don't think I fell asleep but I wasn't sure—everything tangled and tugging—everything pulling me under like weighted nets. Now I knew *the holder* was my mother. I told myself it didn't matter.

You don't come from other people really you may have noticed. I don't mean your body doesn't come from other bodies. I mean you find a myth—a fairy tale—like a hermit crab finds an empty shell on the shore—to crawl inside and live in. You come from the thorny wood—the house at the edge of the thorny wood—you come from the castle—you come from the peasant village at the edge of The Sea of Foreboding or the city beneath The Peak of Impending Fire. The queen is kind or ruthless. A savior arrives or not to steal you from the tower in which you're trapped. You make your way with little light from a twisted house or toward one. You go where you should not go because you must. You pay the price or you get away. You learn and forget or learn and remember. Desire scrawls its hurried name in passing—a path that shifts and jars like a child's cursive—a name not quite your own but the best that you can write. You do not come from others. You come from this.

Eventually I got up—turned my flashlight on—pulled my folding straight razor from my pocket and cut a single button from each of the two mattresses—the most basic white buttons you've ever seen—nothing to commend them but their use—utterly unbeautiful—but not to me. I put them in my pocket and I left that room and I went down those concrete stairs as quickly as I could and I crossed the parking lot trying to remember—anything at all—of that journey years before to my father's house. So much of the city was not the way it was. I set out into the night.

You want to think you've become a different person by growing older—stronger—more sure—but when you're lost in the dark you're always the same—you're always the same when you're back in the frigid water under the ice. *That* night was *this* night—*that* lostness *this* lostness—*that* pavement *this* pavement—*those* steps were *these* steps.

If there's one thing I know it's two things—you can't protect people from the life they want—or yourself from loving them.

KNIFE-THROWER

We travelled by train incessantly—as if the Furies themselves were in pursuit. *Today you will be the girl on the spinning wheel and I'll be the knife-thrower* he said as we boarded a train. *Show them the scars—but only reluctantly and only when asked repeatedly—the cardboard-box-fort scars—and we'll say that's where I missed. They may ask me—How can you live with yourself—they may ask—having never even once put at stake the thing they love the most. I will turn to you and you will tell them you'd have it no other way—you'll say you wouldn't know how else to feel alive. I found her abandoned in a train station*—my father would tell the strangers across from us—*you can't ask anyone to do this who has family. My marriage was built on knives—my wife died doing the thing she loved.*

You arrive from all sides suddenly—like panic or plots against you—you walk into my afternoons my mornings my evenings my nights—you present yourself all at once as if walking through walls or I turn any corner and you are there or I am almost asleep and you enter or I am in the kitchen doing dishes and you are there beside me suddenly.

I sentenced you to death in absentia. I sentenced you to rocks in your pockets in the river—I sentenced you to fire without forgiveness—fierce fire relentless fire starting at your feet—I placed you against the wall—I stood you over the trap under the noose—I marched you into winter—I threw you over cliffs—I buried you alive. You came back again and again. I threw you overboard of my life—into the rushing wake the days leave—the thoughtless spent seconds—the self-shuffling self-dealing deck of hours—into the torrent and still you stood—there in my life.

In my heart I fall down a flight of stairs every time I think of you —every time the same stairs over and over. I fall down a flight of stairs—no railings—no landings—just bruising and breaking again and again.

RETURN

There in the night I walked from the Starry Bright—walked and walked—the way you walk when the wind is hard against you. The streetlights—faint and far apart—flickered and hummed. I stumbled often. Gathered myself. Kept going.

Don't ask when *the holder* came for *what was hers*—or when she pushed me out to live on my own. I can't fill all these endless empty blanks just to keep you listening.

SOMETHING IS SPARED

Sometimes something does not break—the glass you drop—the faucet you force—the screw you turn with too small a Phillips-head. Once in a while something does not break—something you drop on the ground holds itself together—something you toss to the curb—something you step on in a hurry—step on full-weight in a rush to get somewhere. Sometimes something is spared. You can't know why.

The day would come when I would not become the person my father said I would become that day.

UNDER THE ICE

The sky was ricochet-red. We were on a train. He was playing rock paper scissors with a boy sitting opposite us. I needed to find a way to breathe—like that time you were looking for that opening under the ice and you'd found it before again and again but this time you weren't sure and you'd read somewhere that there was the thinnest layer of air between the water and the ice and you pressed your lips there trying to breath in that narrow space and the underside of the ice was burning your lips and your lungs were pulling the air in very slowly like someone greedy trying to gather things unnoticed.

RETURN

Shards in the streets you have to walk with care. A zigzag walk like a children's game of being drunk. The darkness seemed to deepen. The streets to lengthen. No one followed. No one lurked. No cause for alarm. No panic. A few men milled unmenacingly —nightshift workers on break maybe—smoking outside a small factory. You don't want to think as you walk trying to find your way but you can't help it. I thought about my friend—how one Scissor Day I went to The Castaways to tell her she could not be my friend anymore. The Castaways was gone. No sign it had ever been there. Just another vacant lot. Just like her to shuffle off out of my life and leave no forwarding address—just like her. I thought of *the holder*—that wrecking ball stranger who ransacked my life. I thought of my father—*where are you* I thought—*where are you*—how he began to connect the dots that were not there—like fires leap highways in high winds—insistently—so if you disagreed it was like walking into that blackberry bramble at the back of your yard—you were going to get torn up at least a little—maybe a lot. That time you played Russian roulette with no bullets. How many times did you check the cylinder? When you connect the dots that are not there you are never going to get all the bullets out.

Just so you know—my father never struck me. Not even once. It was more the way the drowning wrap themselves around you as they sink. You know nothing remains itself for long in the sea—you know how whole things fragment in the currents in the tides in the riptides in the undertow in the waves in the battering waves.

Distracted I took a wrong turn down a dark side street that led to a chain-link fence adorned with concertina wire. Rusted tracks—paved over in places—ran along the back of what once had been a warehouse. I turned and retraced my steps—reached for my Aspergum—bitter orange.

Sometimes life seems less the sum of the choices you've made and more the remainder of the subtractions you've endured. You know the edge of the sea is not an edge like the razor-cut you made in the cardboard boxes—it is like the edge of something torn. One afternoon I opened the back of my father's gold pocket watch—the one from the pawnshop on Shunt Street—looking for an inscription or initials or something like that. The works were clogged with sand.

TELLING THE TRUTH

Slowly I started to tell myself the truth. It wasn't because I meant to. It happened like counting backwards from z to j or 99 bottles or how many fingers if I count the seconds one-one-thousand two-one-thousand and on and on but really it's more like learning something with your hands that you're never going to forget. And you find out that telling the truth is like settling a score—because to settle a score you must know your way. You don't meander. Something is going to get settled the way that time you were finished with that friend that no good friend who didn't call and didn't call and you were the one who had to carry that weight that weight of waiting that weight of always weighing the costs and when you get finished with that you are done and that is that or that bad friend you've been to yourself and why did you keep waiting to be a better friend and finally you just give up. But if you can't live with yourself anymore how do you move out you want to know. Tell yourself the truth. That's how it happens.

PRETENDING TO BE BLIND

You know you can't side with the sea and not land in the deep. One morning my father pretended to be blind. He said he woke up not being able to see. We were in some town in Eastern Europe somewhere I think. He said I'd have to do everything for him—lead him everywhere—find food—make plans—map routes—bring things he needed to the little house we'd borrowed. I didn't know how to catch or hold the weights that fell from everywhere at once—like bricks from a coming-down house—first thinking how to dodge them—only later asking what I could make of them. My father was good at pretending to be blind—the edge of disbelief and desperation—the shocked suddenness of it on his face—the sudden grabby needy *help me help me* thing he hooked me with. I was swallowed whole. What I could make of it was this—*now it's all up to me*. Later my father forgot the whole thing and started to see again. I did not forget the whole thing.

FREEZING

If you think of water as something that has shattered in your hands and is falling through—that is what it is like when I think of you—like cupping my hands harder and harder to hold what cannot be held. That is what it is like and every day is that day over and over and there is nothing that will make the shattered water whole but freezing—freezing my hands—freezing my heart—freezing everything so everything stops cold.

SALT INTO THE SEA

Sometimes I empty small packets of salt into the sea—the ones I've pocketed in restaurants—the ones with those three little tubes you break open at the top—I break them open and empty them into the sea. Grief is like that too I think—you add in increments to what there is already too much of.

TRACKS

By now the tracks have mostly been torn up—salvaged to make other things—I don't know what.

ROCKS

Sometimes I close my eyes and run my fingers over rocks and trace the hard angles where they've been broken off—and trace the curves where they've been tumbled down rivers—and feel the faint ridges where other rocks have struck them.

TRAINS

We were on a train and my father was debating some point with two men sitting across from us in the compartment—things grew heated and he glanced my way and blurted *I'd wager this girl I found—I mean abducted—I mean adopted—but I've already lost her—Elena—I mean Perdita—to someone else*—and after a pause—*I'm delivering her now to a rug merchant in Edirne*—then he said he'd done it all before and nodded in my direction—*I always escape* I said—*I always find him again on a train somewhere.* The men stared briefly—averted their eyes—turned toward the windows. My father left the compartment to go smoke.

RETURN

I'm trying to work things through—loose ends and dead ends and detours and roadblocks and over the falls in a barrel and through the ice in chains and sometimes a morning so clear it collapses light to a point of fire that makes a fuse of the thousand-mile thread I spool and unspool in my thoughts.

I walk to the center of The Square of Nothing. I begin to scream and scream.

SYMPHONY OF MILES

Sometimes I think I hear trains—especially at night. Once I went out—nearly naked—to follow that sound and find those working tracks—I was running through the streets—my feet scuffed and blistering and torn—I was following that sound—that music of escape—that symphony of miles—how quickly things recede when you seek them in that way—in that *nothing's-going-to-stop-you* kind of way—no pain no harrowing hurt is going to stop you.

RETURN

I stood before my father's house at dawn. In my pocket the Starry Bright buttons slid against and over each other like parts of the past in memory. The slanting light was just as it had been on that morning years ago. All else was changed—the house almost unrecognizable—the block itself foreign as faces in other people's photos. I walked the front porch—looking through curtainless windows into empty rooms. The front yard was untended. Wading through knee-high weeds I went to the back garden—orphaned and wild—that blackberry bramble—tangled like thorned thoughts—now grown over everything. I found my way down some concrete steps to a broken-down basement door and went in. I wandered from room to room—through doorway after doorway. In a corner of the front hall—where the phone table had been—ragged wires protruded from the phone jack—never repaired. The downstairs room where my mother had slept toward the end—saying my father snored but that wasn't it—seemed impossibly small. The second-floor bedrooms were empty as ice. I went to my old room. Stood in front of its single window. Felt nothing.

ROCK

When you run the tips of your fingers across a rock there is always a slightly sandy surface—just barely granular—a barely audible music to the fingers—something you might slide on if you were walking across that rock—if that rock were a slight mountain slope—maybe a canyon below—a river—a sky blue without ceasing—that sense of being situated somehow—of standing on some nearly reliable ground.

TRACKS

They were disassembling the train as it rolled down the tracks—looking for contraband and taking bribes not to see it. After that business about losing me in a bet—sitting there with those strangers—the air closed in like clingwrap. I had to leave the compartment and I found my father standing on the *do not stand here* platform between cars smoking a cigarette and watching the scenery fly by and I wanted to reach for something I couldn't reach like when you reach for something that can't be had by reaching.

MIDNIGHT AS A SECOND LANGUAGE

I climbed the bare attic stairs as I had countless times before. My father would wake me—always at midnight—and I'd follow him up these steep stairs to the room above. I sat on the narrow landing—my back to the closed attic door. I'd sat here before.

SHRED-PAPER RIVER

The night of the company party my father did not wake me at midnight. I woke myself. I put on my socks and climbed these stairs. The door was closed. I sat on this landing listening. In the room on the other side my father was crying and tearing papers to pieces.

It breaks my bones to think of you. It breaks my bones like the compression of a vice—and nowhere to turn held so tight and being crushed—and how are you in there pressing from all sides—how did I ever let you in to break my bones.

PAPER PERSON

When you are a person of paper—when you are a paper person—when you are not a rock or scissors person—you can be crushed and folded and formed and written-on and erased. When you do not smash things—cut things—weigh things down—sever what was once a single thing—when you are flat and thin and your edges are easily found and tucked and creased and made into things and other things like birds or fish or games of choice or games of chance—if you are a paper person you are going to be worked—you are going to comply with the hands of those who work you as they wish—you are not going to easily recognize yourself after those who handle you are through with you. If you are a paper person—at some point—you learn to start to fold yourself—you start to run the flat-sided pencil-edge across your creases to make them sharp—you see that person to please will be pleased if you are a bird—a fish—a star—you are just out ahead of what they will shortly want—you are just in front of what they need—want—wish for—have use of—what they will hold like hands hold hammers—chisels—knives. People smashing things people cutting things apart—the paper people flat and ready and blank—stained—written on—crumpled creased folded pocketed—where do the words go—not to scissors—not to rocks—promises—memories—agreements—who holds them—those of paper—those less solid less keenly edged—those marked with the metal casings of spent erasers—those typed-on—transcribed upon—sisters to beaches scored with tide-lines—sisters to wind-blown plains—to wind-formed clouds—to deserts—sands stacked on sands—words stacked on words—words pressed to paper—words that keep the things of the world from being forgotten.

MIDNIGHT AS A SECOND LANGUAGE

The attic door felt welded shut. The way warped things are always welded shut. I shouldered my weight against it and slid sideways through a narrows—I swear—thin as the line of light the attic window cast across the floor—cleaving the room to halves. The train room smelled like moths to me—the scent of dust and flight—but no dust in the train room—no cobwebs—as if the room were sealed—as if the darkness on the other side were the darkness we had loved—as if the light at my feet were the light we'd fled. The room was a single open space running the length of the house. Exposed beams slanted from a high ceiling down to straight walls. A single window faced east. The plank floor—once covered in scattered Turkish rugs—was rough.

The train room walls were exactly as they'd been—hung like walls of the lost with things to remind you—photos from books and magazines—ripped and scattered across this floor that night—shred-paper puzzles my father left for me to work out—taped back together so meticulously you'd hardly know they'd ever been torn to bits—route maps and schedules—tracks stretching across deserts toward distant mountains—plush compartments—dining cars—mail cars—cabooses—conductors in starched uniforms—photos of tunnels blown through thick rock—trestles—switch-yards—tidy rural stations and grand stations in great capitals jammed with passengers driven against and through each other the way arrivals and departures drive lives through and against the world.

There were stars in the train room ceiling—some now detached and dangling—the ones we'd hung in clusters and constellations—standing on ladders high in that sky—passing the strands of tiny white lights between us—fingers aching with pressing the tacks into place. A painted halfmoon rose on the horizon. In a far corner a distant comet shone. *Under the comet the world ends*—my father had said—*or so the ancients thought*. The room was empty now. I stood where our worn leather chairs had been—next to the saw-horse plywood tables we'd built in stages and drilled for wiring that would make its own tangled underworld beneath the vast layout. My father would push the lever of the black transformer—sparks and magic—and the trains would run into the night from town to town and country to country—our travels all over the world.

I sat on the train room floor—in the silence and changing light. This was the light that woke me sometimes—curled in my chair where my father had left me asleep in the night. I'd get up in the glare—crimped and blinking—stumble toward the stairs—try not to slip in my socks and tumble down.

SIDEWAYS WORLD

I left the house—walked with some effort downtown to the Pharoah Building. Sometimes Dr. Winker stands me up. I sit in the waiting room for what seems forever then I knock and go into his office. I know he's in the building because his glasses are on his desk and his notepad and his blue mechanical pencil. Everything can be erased I think he thinks. Maybe I've lost track of the days again. Maybe the hours are all wrong the way they are sometimes. Maybe he just forgot and took a walk. Maybe he's finished with me but doesn't know how to say so. Back on the street—narrowing myself to fit between people who won't move over—narrow as the silver that backs a mirror—pressed from all sides—into that sideways world between people on their way.

And by the way you simply have to take my word for everything because why else am I talking to you? You're so concerned about everything standing in little rows like school children shoved into lines by rules that override their wild selves and marshal them into silence and taking turns and raising their hands and crushing into chairs between speeches and shrill bells. I know you think I knew where my father's house was all along—as if you never hide things from yourself—as if the mysteries you knot and unknot don't have answers staring you in the face. I want you to see things the way I do for once. How each day starts at the Square of Nothing called midnight.

THE BENT AND THE BROKEN

Deep in the dark I returned to my father's house and up the narrow stairs and through the crack in the door and sat on the train room floor where my chair had been and closed my eyes and let the tangled world go.

All things bent are blessed to have not been broken. All things broken are blessed to not live bent.

We were on a train. My father was playing rock paper scissors with the little boy sitting across from us in the compartment—it was all very light and giddy—but then—after a while—my father would not play by the rules—he said *The rock and scissor people will always beat the paper people no matter what the game rules say—the people who let themselves be folded and crumpled and tossed away and written on at will and erased and marked through and written on again and cut and scarred and scored—these people who leave it to everyone—anyone—to tell them who they are—no rock—no scissor—ever is like that.* And the little boy soon understood that paper was not a winning choice and that rock still smashed scissors and soon the two were all clenched fists slamming against each other and the little boy became frenzied and fierce and his unsettled mother had to intervene to stop the game but it was clear that the boy would never forget what he had learned and he sat fidgeting in his seat—restless with what he now knew.

My father left the compartment to have a cigarette between cars. After a minute I followed. He stood on the little platform—his back to me—and there alone in the train room—on that last imagined journey—I flattened my palms like perfect paper sheets and I pushed him from the train.

THE SEA

I could hear the sea in the night as I left the house. The smell of the salt was like the night's second self. I found an unbroken shell at the beach one morning and just an edge was showing at the surface and I dug it out and it shone like wet tortoiseshell and I sat with it in my hands and when I turned it its interior showed itself spiraling deep like some mystery I'd discovered in myself.

MAGIC

Magic means another use for the ordinary. That time you tried to make a music box out of things in the kitchen drawers and the sewing box and the drawers in your parent's bedroom—a music box with gears that interlaced with little plucking prongs that made a song you heard as if from far away—or long ago—when you still searched for music in ordinary things.

Sometimes magic is not a single thing—a right away thing—something isn't magic at the start is what I'm trying to say. Maybe some things become magic because someone risks something to bring the magic out—the way you bring something out of a building about to collapse. Maybe some things only become magic when you give them away.

STREETCAR

In the fairy tale—that which could never happen happens nonetheless—to you—even as your logic papers magic over with cause and effect in the domino world of tiles striking tiles to make a life of everything fallen over. Something happens in your life—something that blazes—like a comet in the sky—something that puts the lie to all that is fixed and forgone. Even as it happens you know that this event will stand like a wall at the back of your life—at the back of everything—that everything that comes after will stand apart from everything gone before—an event whose remnants will always stand in your path—an event that will never be over.

What happened was this—I took the streetcar to the edge of the *Leap Year River Bridge*—I was taking my cookie tin of favorite buttons to dump them in the river. Sometimes you have to look at something one last time before you're done with it—you have to look even though you know that you must not. Things you've hidden can be that way as well—you have to really look at them—before you stop hiding them. Anyway I started to pry the lid off of that tin—I've told you before what this was like—*slowly*—*more slowly still*—one last look then I would exit the streetcar quickly and dump the buttons straightaway from that bridge and I would not look down to see them tumbling down into the current and I would leave and I would not look back and I would go into the city and collect all the buttons I'd hidden in all the abandoned buildings and throw them into river after river until they were all gone. On the streetcar—sitting on a bench seat—in the dim light and indifference—I worked the lid of that tin and when it blew off like something under pressure everyone turned and the buttons rose in the air like some confetti storm and then they fell and struck the floor—some flat—some skidding—many rolling on their edges everywhere—and the people on the streetcar—as if they had never seen anything colorful fall at their feet—rose up astonished and laughing and bending and grabbing and talking to each other and it was a miracle like the first struck match—there before my eyes—as if the spell of the glass-eyed blind had been broken by beauty.

I didn't keep my appointment with Dr. Winker that day—or ever again. And something more—before I forget to tell you—the people who pocketed buttons on that streetcar—I never saw them again—any of them—as if they'd found a way out—as if the buttons were tickets of escape.

THINGS BECOME WHAT THEY NEVER WERE

You know how weathered wood can seem hard as steel—wood you can't drive a nail into no matter what? How does that happen exactly I'd like to know. How do things become what they never where? It happens all the time in different ways I've come to see. That which was alive will be what it was not when it is dead. We know this for sure. But redemption—transformation—in that swirl of continuous motion—is always just underneath I think—as long as you are alive. So I thought that the glass-eyed blind could see again.

WHERE SPARKS FLY OUT

I tried it on that the entire underworld was in my care—and those who walked its streets—and the words they spoke to themselves—puzzling through this place as if it were a place they'd never been—like every day's a place you've never been until you talk its unfamiliarity away. I tried it on that these were in my care—but not as if I were something at the center—not like suns wield planets—but more in that way that when you see something—for what it really is—that thing is in your care. I tried it on that I could change everything. I held that thought like a blade against a grinding wheel where sparks fly out as the sharpening takes shape—as the sparkling sheer edge emerges from pared metal where the less of it there is the more toward its purpose it is made ready—like Scissor Day—where purpose is exacted through subtraction—just like that.

BUTTONS

You can walk through the whole city without being seen if you know the route—alleyways—hidden stairways—in and out of side doors—through abandoned buildings—under underpasses—up fire escapes—along rooftops—through what were once great gardens now overgrown—on paths of rough stone like walking the spine-bones of beasts—you can move through the city unseen if you know the way.

I retrieved the buttons I'd horded in building after building. I slipped them through car windows left cracked in the heat. I put them in people's mailboxes. I dropped them into people's pockets on buses. I pinned them to people's clothes on clotheslines behind their houses. I put them behind wipers on windshields. I tucked them in the folds of napkins at restaurants.

I looked for the intervals in the lives of people moving through this city—the gaps between parts of plans—between sentences—between footsteps—where something could be placed—something unexpected—something simple and small and beautiful—to force the reinterpretation of everything. I started dropping buttons here and there—into those sudden spaces—spaces like the distances you see in people's eyes—into the silences at bus stops—into the pockets of strangers—into the hands of beggars—from balconies and mezzanines—from the opened windows of buildings soon to be demolished—sometimes with precision—sometimes by chance—sometimes just for this person—sometimes for anyone.

I gave buttons to those who were waiting. I gave buttons to the busy—those caged in gated hours like people passing through checkpoints without end. I gave buttons to the fearful—fears like blinders—fears pressed into lives like cylinders pressed into wax.

I gave buttons to those alone in narrow spaces—spaces collapsed around them like burned down houses.

Somewhere in the teeth of being trapped there is a doorway—an interval—some reckoning with a crossroads in the woods or in the sand or in yourself. You know what I mean—I know you do—you've stood at those points of reckoning—you've crossed that empty space that breaks the grip of that person you have to leave—of that city that once was yours but now is not—of that job that chokes you like smoke when there's a fire in the house you can't find and can't put out—and you found that single second—or even that space between seconds—and you went sideways between those teeth that had torn and trapped you and you freed yourself and you fled.

Slowly the city started to empty out. Even the gods can't stop what has to happen.

THE LAST SCISSOR DAY

On the last Scissor Day I stood by my living room window watching the street. Soon *the holder* would arrive like a blast of wind from an open window in winter—stingy as pinched salt she'd drop the cold food packets and bitter tea on the counter in the empty kitchen. I'd hated her like weight hates height but none of that mattered now. The thing about getting out of the underworld is this—you have to get everyone else out first. I'd leave one of the Starry Bright buttons—it didn't matter which—on the short narrow table in the dining room.

I went to the bedroom. I pulled my tin with its last few buttons from under my bed and put it in a pocket on the inside of my coat. I lifted the mirror of the dead onto my back—tied it with clothesline cord—the mirror facing skyward—carried it through the streets—carefully so not to fall and everything be broken—to the *Zig Zag River Bridge*. I stood on that bridge—the mirror on my back reflecting the sky.

Slowly I started to tell myself the truth. You can't destroy the mirror of the dead on some Scissor Day—you can't throw it off the *Zig Zag River Bridge*—because on the far other side of its newly re-silvered surface—are the living. I went back to the mirror-works on Midwick Street. The one where I hid my backpack you'll remember. Everywhere old instruction manuals lay in stacks—old tools and chemicals—dusty and abandoned. I think I told you there weren't any mirrors there—none anywhere—just empty frames where mirrors had been or were going to be. I fumbled through manual after manual—looking for instructions for re-silvering a mirror. These I found. This is not child's play. This is not a casual thing you manage halfheartedly on some afternoon when you're bored and slightly distracted. You take the backing of the mirror off—there are diagrams with dotted lines and arrows—you can't be casual about this kind of thing—you are unclouding the mirror with poisons with acids with corrosives—you are clearing the mirror at your peril—you are told not to breathe while clearing the mirror—you are told not to open your eyes—you are instructed to wear gloves to wear goggles to wear masks—you are told to find air so the fumes do not overtake you—you are instructed step by step in the hazards of bringing the mirror back to life. Sometimes I'd fall asleep—the manuals spread around me like kid's books in a dentist's office—you know—something to distract them from the drilling yet to come. Sometimes I'd just sit on the broad-planked floor with all the things around me simply standing.

You know how sometimes everything falls away—all the inside scaffoldings—all the things that hold things in their place among other things—and things are just standing there—just there as they are—without the threads that tie them to other things—that's what I'm trying to say about how I'd sit on the floor of the mirror-works and everything would just be standing there beside me.

CLEARED MIRROR

When the mirror was finally cleared I stood before it like one of those standing-there things. It was like someone I'd be in the future—walking through a doorway to meet me—the expression of non-recognition on both our faces. I was thinner than I'd thought. Taller too. Less pale. I watched my fingers touch my face like you'd touch some foreign thing you'd wondered about. They brushed the crooked bridge of my nose—my lips—the edge of my jaw. My cheeks were lightly lined. My teeth looked like they didn't know which way to turn. My hair was ash and dust. My eyes were dark-place blue. It was cold. The cold truth I guess it was.

Every minute I'd thought of my father was a minute my father had stolen from my life. Every minute I'd thought of him was a minute when something substantial could have been at stake—when something actual could have been grasped and lifted and brought into my life.

BONFIRE

I hid the tin of buttons under the backpack and I left the mirror-works and on my way out I grabbed a can of some sort of flammable liquid—you know—with flames on the mostly illegible label and the grooved twist top cap that you can't unscrew without your fingers burning like scalding water—and I walked the many blocks back to my almost empty house. I pulled my mattress down the stairs and the last chair and the last plate and the last cup and the last of my clothes from the closet and the rat-murder-window fan and the atlas and the short narrow dining table and the button was gone and I knew I'd never see *the holder* again. In the middle of the street I piled these last few things and doused them with that accelerant from the mirror-works and lit them and let them burn and burn and I turned and left that fire untended and I left that empty house for the last time and I walked to Siren Beach.

THE SEA

I slept by the sea—away from every doorway. The sea is like a stranger at your door. Even if you turn and go inside it does not leave—it never ever ceases at your doorstep—pouring itself over itself—into itself—making and remaking its long continuous sentence that you know is no sentence at all it is so close and undisclosing—like being alive. I sat on the sand in the dark—facing the sea—and in the sea I saw myself from the outside-in—everything tumbling and widening and contracting and sweeping itself from underneath itself and positing and retracting and no thing steady and no thing constant and my volition like some engine connected to nothing. There by the sea—on the cold sand—curled up like a shell—I wondered if things retrieved are things made new—the way I've heard that memories are always made from scratch.

I thought how death's message was *Notice what's missing*—where death stands in a doorway—forgetting all who have passed and in that forgetting they are gone—and that in that noticing of the missing was the doorway out of that forgetting—the doorway back. There by the sea—on the cold sand—shivering like sails—I woke and rose and brushed myself off and walked from the sea past house after house.

TOUCHING NOTHING

I reached *the holder*'s house and broke in easily. In that house of the thousand things—I touched nothing. I walked among the shelves and laden tables and framed pictures as one walks among predators. You know that city from that fairy tale—that fairy tale you tell yourself about your past—that city you come back to and everything you remember and everything you've forgotten is in that city out of order stacked in heaps stuffed in corners jammed together the way you think it's going to be when you take your last breath and your life falls all at once in all its dissevered parts through that field of vision inside yourself that soon will be starless—moonless—without meteors—but for those last few minutes you will be in the inundation zone of all that you have seen and heard and felt and wondered about. Standing in that house—walking its rooms and halls across the train room rugs—was just like that.

I touched nothing of those thousand hoarded things—those things of the gods that they had been denied—those things withheld from Scissor Days—all hoarded for herself. I knew this past like you know the face of someone you've forgotten—maybe even your own face from long ago—in a photograph maybe—by a lake or in front of a building—maybe you are standing next to someone—you have no idea who they are—who they were—who they were to you or why they were standing there—a past like that is what I'm talking about—where at first you don't find yourself in that photograph. I know that you know what I mean.

A desk was covered with letters—spread out like opened fans—return addresses removed from every one—cleanly cut away I think with the small silver scissors on the red lacquer tray—some maybe from my other mother—maybe with some money and some suggestions for my care—some maybe from my father—about the new life he'd made—where he'd been—what he'd been doing all these years—I touched none of them—opened none of them—left them where they were. Among the many pictures were framed photos of them together—my father and *the holder*. In one he'd arched his arm just so to block the sun—the shadow hiding his eyes like a bandit mask. In another it seemed he'd sort of married her—like he'd sort of parented me—and it looked to be a hastily arranged affair—a kind of plastic flowers matrimony—no one to witness it maybe—or maybe just someone yanked from the hotel bar.

I did not linger for hours—I did not linger at all. When I left that house I left it like you walk from some place finally. I did not burn that house to the ground. I did not smash things—crush things under heels—turn tables over. You don't have to destroy everything you're finished with.

THINGS LEFT

I walked the long empty avenues—past empty closed-curtained houses—toward the mirror-works. At the mirror-works I lifted the re-silvered mirror onto my back again and tied it again with clothesline cord and grabbed my tin of buttons and my backpack by its straps and I walked through the empty streets to the Square of Nothing and I left the tin and the mirror at its center—things for the next to arrive.

THE SECOND LANGUAGE OF LEAVING

I boarded the bus at midnight—as a second language—the second language of leaving—the one I'd been trying to speak to myself through the closed doors of closed days. I boarded the bus at midnight—as a doorway opposite the doorway of the dead—in the intervals—through a sideways crack in the world.

Every origin—every escape from hell—is an act of imagination—that's the point.

In the vacant lot where the terminal had been the driver stood by the door of the idling bus collecting fares. He asked where I wanted to go. I pulled the pink and black beaded map from my pocket—unfolded it—handed it to him—and I gave him my father's watch from the pawnshop for payment. He wondered if it worked. I knew it didn't. He looked me in the eyes and bounced it in his hand as if to weigh it. He seemed to be waiting—like someone waiting for someone to finish a sentence. I palmed the Starry Bright button and turned my pockets inside out to show that they were empty. He nodded—signaled me to board. The bus smelled like the Pix I think before it was abandoned—that smell of public use—a place where people sit and wait and watch. We pulled out. The side of my face pressed against cold glass. I fell asleep.

UNDER THE COMET

Under the comet the world ends. So the Ancients thought. They were not wrong. Under the comet we walked into the sea. Hand in hand. That slow heavy striding like horses fording deep water—that sense of the muscular—present as dull pain. Under the comet the world ends. Beneath the dome of storms we strode into the sea—steady as horses. You can't think outside of action like this. Action like this is its own thinking. Muscular. Heavy as horses. Our hands lightly locked. In the surf costs weigh themselves on either side with every step. The tilting balances—the blurred fulcrum unfixed—a life squared to hold whole oceans back—the sunken drives stirring and rising like breath sprung from depths—the costs accumulate—collide like punches—rapid as stressed hearts. The walls fall forward. Until they fall you don't know what they hide.

RAIN

I woke with a start. The rain sounded like thousands of snapping sticks—like the stick-house of my life coming down. *Memory is a fire made only for rain* my father had said. Now I knew that Lethe was not a river at all—it was a downpour—and in that deluge was a doorway beyond which stretched the arid streets of the underworld and the underworld's tidal lock on those who walked them. And I saw how every doorway is a standing rainless replica of that vertical river of forgetting—that river that divides the world from the underworld.

THE OUTSIDE THINGS

On the other side of that storm—at dawn—the horizon flared like a fire-clock. We jerked in the jostle and rumble of a rutted dirt road. The bus made its way unevenly toward some ghost town or outpost on the outskirts of some desert. Across the hills wildflowers bloomed and by the roadside creosote bush swayed in steady wind. Within an hour we ground to a halt in front of a bleached yellow clapboard house with scattered outbuildings corrals and a falling-down barn. Someone from the middle of the bus rose—grabbed a canvas bag from above her seat—strode down the aisle and left the bus.

After so long of not being able to see the outside things—the landscape lay before me. The foothills looked like coral reefs laid bare when the tide withdraws before a tidal wave—all streaked with strata—iron—copper—manganese—limestone—sandstone—jasper. Everything was different now—different in that way that things are different from the inside out—so someone else might see things just the same but for you everything is changed. Spells having been broken I think is what's most like what I'm talking about—what I'm trying to say—the spell of forgetfulness broken.

THE LIFE I HAVE

Through the bus window the landscape steadied me. The pinball ricochet of narratives—images—voices—grew father apart like the towns. Then stopped.

The bus paused at random spots along the way—not really stations as such but simply places by the road or down some street or at some house. Passengers departed one by one and I remained as the bus emptied out. We stopped for half an hour in a nameless town far from everything—much of the downtown storefronts were boarded up—on a corner was an out-of-business hair salon in a building that once housed a bank. I got off the bus and walked into a graveyard by a rundown church—sat with my back to a gravestone—ate some squeeze-cheese and a pepperoni stick—wildflowers everywhere.

I don't have the life of some other person—I only have the life of the person I am. Maybe this is what remembering means—having your self at hand like knowing where to reach to pick something up—like you know the scissors are in the drawer and you don't even notice how your hand so quickly finds them. I've never had a way to reach for my self like that—always just drawers full of random things—always shuffling through everything for so long I'd forget what I'd been looking for. Maybe this has happened to you every now and then so you know what it feels like to just be rummaging almost without purpose through everything.

Town after town—street after street after street—side streets—alleyways—people standing on corners—standing in stores—walking side-by-side or walking alone—tracing the tidal lock of paper scissors rock—habits they can't turn from—tasks—familiar circuits transcribing their steps—steps just steps removed from lives they could have led.

NEEDLES

The bus did not go to Needles. It rattled into some desert town toward dusk and down a side street and then the driver stopped—glanced in his rearview mirror—muttered *end of the line* and signaled me to exit.

I was left facing three vacant lots in a row between two slightly rundown houses—one empty—one seeming to maybe be occupied. Midway between the houses—in the dust and rocks and stubble—someone had set up a folding chair—you know one of the cheap aluminum kind with the multicolored nylon straps—now long faded—and beside it sat a coffee can partly filled with cigarette butts. No street sign. No house numbers. It didn't matter. Dust from the U-turned bus blew past. I sat down in that chair and watched the light begin to withdraw from the sky and felt the temperature ratcheting down notch by notch.

Maybe everything I had folded so carefully into shape—folded like an origami swan—into itself to become itself and clear—was not at all what finally was the case—the case in the world. Maybe it didn't matter where I was—maybe it was just that I had arrived at this place—this place far from all I had constructed. Sometimes when you come to the end of things there is a stillness. Sometimes the end of things is like a narrows you've traveled and at its end there is a broadening. After a while I rose and walked down the dusty street to where it ended in the sand. I waded through sage and rabbit brush to a clearing. The falling stars were darting across the sky—brief as fireflies—briefer. Another year and another—ramming into remnants—fragments—whole things.

STARRY BRIGHT

I held the Starry Bright button tightly in my hand. It was hard and circular like that decision you have to live with over and over—the one that pulls you ceaselessly back-and-forth like the sea—the one locked from inside—deadbolt after deadbolt—shouldered again and again—that vice-tightened thing in yourself that locks you out and locks you in.

There in that broad stillness I found my actual voice—right there—and it surfaced like someone coming up for air from under the ice when the ice has thawed. I spoke to the sage—the rabbit brush—the night. *I know you don't know me but I have come a long way—from the underworld actually—and now I remember everything—and I know I have returned to the world and I want you to stand with me because I don't want to stand alone.*

THE DOOR THAT CANNOT BE CLOSED

I know my father walked into the sea. When someone you have loved walks into the sea—any sea—I mean kills themselves—a door is opened in your life that cannot be closed. You can't see into the room on the other side—you can't go in—because it's not really a room. You will live with this door in your life—this door that cannot be closed and cannot be entered. It shows up in room after room—on any wall—at any time—in the middle of a sentence—in a glance over someone's shoulder—in a garden—on a highway—always exactly the same. This door that stands in your life—that cannot be talked shut—bricked over—papered over—turned from. This door that time can't out-wait—you will face it again and again—because on this door's other side—time is not.

UNDER THE COMET

That last midnight—under the comet—into a gathering storm—we walked to Siren Beach. How he suddenly just kept walking—into the waves—of course I'd go with him—into the waves and under the sea forever.

You know how strange it is when things you think you've chosen stack up on the other side of the fulcrum and begin to lift you from the ground? How do you reweight your life from a place like that—the chain of days so stacked against you—how do you reweight your entire life in a single act?

When you cut with a razor blade or a carpet knife or some other kind of knife you are supposed to cut away from yourself but you can't always cut away from yourself sometimes you must cut toward yourself when the thing you are trying to cut is thick or long or hard-to-cut and sometimes you have to cut toward yourself in other ways when life gives you things to cut that you cannot safely cut.

I cut toward myself in the waves—in the gale—in the undertow. I cut toward myself as I slipped my hand from his lightly closed hand and I cut toward myself as I turned and I cut toward myself with every heavy slogging stride toward shore and I cut toward myself by not looking back and not letting anything pull me back and with every slicing sobbing disbelieving breath I cut toward myself with all my strength—in the rain in the blowing rain—in my making my way to shore.